RESET

RESET

REGAINING INDIA'S ECONOMIC LEGACY

SUBRAMANIAN SWAMY

RUPA

Published by
Rupa Publications India Pvt. Ltd 2019
7/16, Ansari Road, Daryaganj
New Delhi 110002

Sales Centres:
Allahabad Bengaluru Chennai
Hyderabad Jaipur Kathmandu
Kolkata Mumbai

ISBN: 978-93-5333-651-6

First impression 2019

10 9 8 7 6 5 4 3 2 1

Printed at Replika Press Pvt. Ltd, India

CONTENTS

Preface: India: In Search of a Renaissance   *vii*

1. Imperialism Uproots Agriculture   1

2. Industrialization: Missed Opportunities   21
   and Unfulfilled Promises

3. The Albatross around India's Economic Neck:
   The Soviet Model   40

4. Roar of the 'Caged' Tiger   87

5. A Tryst with Destiny That Never Materialized   103

6. The Modi Years: Looking Back, Looking Ahead   132

Appendix: Towards a New Ideology of Integral Humanism   173

Index   191

PREFACE

India: In Search of a Renaissance

In the autumn of 1969, I returned to India after a seven-year stay in the United States (US). The first two years were spent in getting a PhD from Harvard University, whereafter I joined the Harvard faculty for five years to teach Economics to graduate and undergraduate students. Upon my return to India, I joined the Indian Institute of Technology (IIT), Delhi, as a Professor of Economics. But soon after, I ran into a controversy around socialist planning, which was then the official policy. I challenged the then conventional wisdom that socialist planning was a superior route for economic progress as compared to a competitive market economy. I also questioned whether social justice was optimized through socialist redistribution of income by progressive taxation and nationalization, rather than by a rapid growth in the gross domestic product (GDP) caused by encouraging investment through incentives, and based on innovation, and through employment generation.

I also felt there was a third way of economic development which would harmonize a number of objectives, such as growth, social justice and creating room for spiritual values. Both socialism and market economy are purely materialist, and that suits the West, but it does not suit Indian culture, which venerates sacrifice and simple living. Hence, I wrote a monograph[1] titled *Swadeshi Plan* in 1970, which was presented on the floor of the Lok Sabha by Atal Bihari Vajpayee, the then Parliamentary leader of the Bharatiya Jana Sangh. The monograph was an instant hit in the country, partly because during the Budget session of 1970, Mrs Indira Gandhi, as the prime minister, ridiculed the monograph on the floor of the Parliament. She said that the Plan had 'overambitious goals' and referred to me as 'Santa Claus'. The political influence and blackmail of the Soviet Union to obtain intellectual compliance for Soviet planning, however, was so strong that few dared then to speak up against the futility of Indians continuing with the Soviet model. However, since I did, the establishment, following Mrs Gandhi's speech, as if on cue, ensured the termination of my professorship at IIT Delhi. The professorship was restored retrospectively two decades later by a Delhi court, but by then, I had become a Cabinet minister. Hence, though I resumed my professorship in March 1991, I resigned the very next day, and also recovered at an 8 per cent interest rate decades of my past unpaid basic salary and other emoluments.

After termination of the professorship in 1972, my ideas on India-specific economic development became part of my lectures around the country. But I could not find the time needed to convert the *Swadeshi Plan* monograph into a book. After years of becoming a Member of Parliament (MP) in 1974, and then combating the Emergency declared by Mrs Gandhi in 1975, it has become possible to devote time for it, and hence this book has now been penned.

In this book, I have, for the period of 150 years from 1870 to

---

[1]Subramanian Swamy, *Indian Economic Planning: An Alternative Approach*, Vikas Publishing, New Delhi, 1971

2019, focused not so much on the historical narrative of India's economic development—or the lack of it—but on distilling out the consequences of the economic ideology adopted in three main phases. First, British imperialism (1870–1947), during which period, according to me, $71 trillion worth of resources was drained off to Britain. Thereafter, the Soviet command economy model took root (1950–90), which ended with the collapse of the Union of Soviet Socialist Republics (USSR) in 1991. Thus, liberation from state commandism came through the economic reforms (1991–2019) initiated by me in 1990–91, and during 1992–96 by assisting P.V. Narasimha Rao while holding a Cabinet rank in his government.

Over the past several millennia of acknowledged civilized history of the world, India—identified globally as Hindustan (or just 'Yindu' to the Chinese long before it was known as 'Hind' to the Arabs)—was, by contemporary standards, the most developed and civilized nation, until AD 1750, by which time foreign aggression had already taken its toll and emaciated India economically. India, thus, as the Global Number 1 economically declined from the end of the twelfth century to become the poorest by 1947.

From 1870 to 1947, British imperialism in India was structured by a policy of killing domestic entrepreneurship, blocking innovations and extracting resources from agriculture through land-revenue collectors called zamindars. The contrast is visible in statistical data of development between the *directly* British-ruled provinces of India and the *indirectly* administered princely states by appointed regents of British imperialists. The damage done by imperialism to India's agricultural performance through arbitrary cruel revenue extraction and siphoning it off to Britain or for local administration contrasts sharply with the economic performance in agriculture of princely states, which had better development and growth rates of output in agriculture. The fact is that foreign-ruled governments which funnel funds out of a nation, as the British government did in India for a century (and could not do in China due to that nation's indigenous governance), wreck all the inter-sectoral balances in the economy and thus destabilize and impoverish the nation.

By bleeding agriculture to the bone, exporting and draining national resources estimated at $71 trillion at current prices, and by blocking native innovation, the British rule set India two centuries back in development. India thus missed the Industrial Revolution. India's industrial development at Independence was spotty and served British trade interests and not the setting up of industrialization in India. By 1947, India, once the world's richest, had become the poorest, with a per capita income of just $150. But India survived, retaining the substance of its ancient culture and religion—unlike nations such as Persia, Egypt, Rome and Greece, which were forced to abandon their culture and convert to the religion and culture of their invaders. India is globally the most prominent exception. It remained defiant and unconverted by foreign rule, despite two major brutal and diabolical foreign onslaughts: one of Muslims and the other of Christian subversion via imperialism, totalling an 800-year span of India's history.

For free India, since 1947, to regain the earlier highest global position, and to recover from the past exploitation and imposed psychological damage, it was first important to reverse the regression and move people from negativity to an optimistic outlook. This required an innovational dynamic mindset of the new Indian leadership. Upon achieving freedom, this negativity began to diminish but very slowly, because after Gandhi's and Patel's untimely deaths, the Nehru government's decision to accept the history of India as written by paid British scholars, such as Max Mueller and his slavish Indian tutees, who had imposed into textbooks falsehoods such as the Aryan-Dravidian racial theory or India as never before one nation, etc., legitimized a slavish mindset for the native Indian. No one has better portrayed this depravity than Dr B.R. Ambedkar in his writings in 1916.[2]

Over the last seven decades, this negativity has, of course, mostly dissipated. During P.V. Narasimha Rao's tenure as the prime minister, the GDP growth rate rose from a four-decade trend rate of 3.5 per cent per year (derisively called 'The Hindu rate of growth' by Left-wing scholars) to 8 per cent per year by 1996. It is regrettable that since then, no government has bettered it. This acceleration in the growth rate of GDP could have come earlier *but did not* and, neither did it come later because the prime ministers of free India made the biggest and most unforgivable mistake by borrowing a wholly inapplicable model from abroad which, before Narasimha Rao, and later, called for neglecting agriculture, to use the inter-sectional terms of trade to finance the setting up of capital-intensive industries in a labour-surplus country. The model failed, and obviously did so because India's agriculture was already bone-dry in 1947 and heavy industry products did not have much of a market within India while exports' possibility was minimal since the developed countries had no use for sub-standard products.

Nevertheless, Indians, after 1996, began to feel for the first time since Independence that India could grow fast and the myth spread by Left-wing and Westernized Indians that the GDP growth rate of India could not exceed 3.5 per cent per year had exploded forever.

---

[2]See Subramanian Swamy, *Hindutva and National Renaissance*, Har-anand Publishers, New Delhi, 2013
Dr Ambedkar, 'Castes in India: Their Mechanism, Genesis and Development', at a seminar in the Anthropology department in Columbia University, New York, 1916

The grip of Soviet influence had continued to prevail from 1950 till 1990 when the new Janata government with Chandra Shekhar as the prime minister and me as the senior-most Cabinet minister began unravelling the Soviet unholy grip. Conveniently for us, the Soviet Union had also unravelled into sixteen separate nations, leaving a rump Russia. With it ended all direct and indirect foreign Soviet and Leftist influence in our economic policymaking.

However, due to a fascination for foreign investment since 2008, the economy has been in steady retrogression, worsening to a fluctuating but declining trend. Since 2016, the economy has dangerously gone into a tailspin. I had predicted that the economy would be in a serious crisis in a series of Op-eds published over four years, especially in *The Hindu* and in public addresses in the country. But the warning was not heeded and hence the nation today is in a difficult situation with most indicators quite depressing to see.

I had no hope from the earlier two United Progressive Alliance (UPA) governments (2004–14), in which Prime Minister Dr Manmohan Singh, though an accomplished economist, remained a marginal figure of no consequence in his own government, and accidentally a prime minister. His government saw some of the most senior ministers committing gigantic corruption, and coming to the adverse notice of the law and undergoing prosecution in courts.

As a prime minister, Narendra Modi is the exact opposite of his predecessor, Dr Singh. He is not a person of letters, and one who has an unstudied familiarity with microeconomics but not macroeconomics and its intricacies of inter-sectoral economic dynamics. But he has immense appeal with the masses and hard-working middle classes, and thus the mandate to carry out major reforms. He is honest in money matters. Moreover, he has come up from his humble beginnings the hard way, by pulling himself up by the boot straps and thus, by example, has won over the toiling masses of India—to win election after election from 2002 onwards, first at the state level as the chief minister and now twice as the prime minister.

But this same lack of academic background has made him dependent on his friends and chosen rootless ministers, who never tell him the bitter truth about the economy or explain the macroeconomics or that he needs to figure the way out of a crisis. Hence, we have witnessed the folly of demonetization and the inanity of the Goods and Services Tax (GST), both of which have accelerated the tailspin of the economy.

But as the prime minister, he is a domineering figure who brooks no political competition. His reliance on unelectable political advisors and colleagues for clues on the complex subject of the economy, which they know little about, or even lettered but timid economists appointed by him to posts of huge perks, results in them telling the prime minister only what he wants to hear. This is a frightening *potpourri* for the nation.

The good news is that the current developing crisis does not necessarily mean an imminent collapse of the economy. That is India's historic innate resilience. To solve the current problems, the first step is to recognize the urgency that a crisis is imminent or already in existence. I have suggested a new menu of measures to stem the tailspin and turn it around to a fast-growing economy. The Bharatiya Janata Party (BJP) government also needs to give an alternative ideological thrust to economic policy rather than trying to improve on the failed efforts in the past and to seek marginal changes. Now is the time for a structural overhaul to purge the remnants of the command economy, and usher in an incentive-driven, innovation-structured and market-determined competitive economy.

The people of this young republic, but an ancient civilization, which is known the world over, are demanding modern transformation and rapid growth within the framework of our ancient values and heritage. Thus, today's India is an ancient nation in search of a renaissance. In the Preamble of the Constitution, our nation is defined as 'India that is Bharat'. The term 'Indian', that is 'Bharatiya', signifies a citizen of the Republic of India. India is a new republic but not a new nation. Its people are modern, but they do not reject the nation's time-tested traditions and the cultural heritage of its age-old past.

Now, in 2019, as a renewed republic entering the eighth decade of Independence, India stands at the cusp of a major transformation caused by unprecedented economic development through out-of-the-box thinking, using everything from primitive tools to electronic software, and from entrepreneurship to hard work and self-confidence. This has given a significant and substantial boost to the quality of life for its more than 1.25 billion citizens. There is now, since Independence, a realistic hope for India to regain its ancient glory, to become the most advanced nation. Its GDP has risen to more than $2 trillion and, in current prices, it is now already the third-largest nation in terms of real GDP (in Purchasing Power Parity [PPP] prices). This rapid growth has created an emerging middle class with rising aspirations and the ability to discover, invent and adapt modern scientific innovations for natural development.

In 2019, India leads the world in the supply pool of youth, i.e., percentage of the young in the age group of 15 to 35 years (about 65 per cent), and this lead is expected to last for another forty years. This young generation, with growing access to quality education, Internet use and mobile connectivity, is not only empowered to demand positive change but is the most fertile milieu for promoting knowledge, innovation and research, which will ensure accentuated, sustainable economic growth in GDP at 10 per cent per year. It is this prime workforce that also encourages saving for the future, thus providing the corpus for pension-funding for the retired and the old. We should, therefore, not squander this 'natural vital resource', termed Demographic Dividend, which will shrink as development proceeds and as quality of life further improves in the future.

India is thus at the inflexion point or cusp in the curve of transformational growth to global power status. India has now regained its position as the fastest-growing large economy in the world, but a 7 per cent GDP growth rate is not good enough any more. Economic growth must accelerate over the next two decades to meet the rising aspirations of our young consumer population. India thus needs to achieve and sustain a GDP growth rate of over 10 per cent per year for the next two decades (2020–40). This sustained GDP growth will be accompanied by an increase in per capita income growth from $1,500 to over $7,000 per year at 2019 prices, and thus make the third angle of the global triangle of India, China and the US.

For this, India must adopt a three-pronged strategy that can create capabilities for growth and new solutions, which will, in turn, build shared prosperity for its 1.25 billion citizens. Firstly, development must become a mass movement, in which every Indian recognizes and experiences tangible benefits accruing immediately, even as long-gestation reforms continue to be implemented. Secondly, our development strategy must help achieve broad-based economic growth to ensure development across all regions and states, and across all sectors, ranging from education, agriculture and healthcare to manufacturing, urbanization and retail/trade. This needs the fostering of new innovations and the upskilling of labour, modernization of agriculture, water resource management, finding new fuel sources (such as thorium), and strong research and development (R&D), and physical infrastructure. These path-breaking innovations have to be backed by robust financial architecture and human resource development.

Finally, our growth strategy must minimize the gap between public- and private-sector performance. This calls for efficient, transparent and accountable state governance, which will require developing rational risk-taking and merit-rewarding governance. This will ensure that India not only achieves its ambitious goals for 2040, of overtaking China, but also challenges the pre-eminence of the US, to go on to become scientifically one of the two largest economies in the world by 2050. Thus, as we would then celebrate the centenary of our republic established in 1950, such a national development effort will enable us to challenge the hegemony of the US, in innovation-driven growth and global order.

This book provides the policy prescription required for India to emerge as the most developed nation once again, and before 2050, but after reviewing the economic history from 1870 and drawing important lessons on how and why we lost our premier developed status over the last 800 years. It will underscore the essential concerted effort required by all stakeholders—viz. the government, business leaders, and intellectuals and other citizens—to deliver this growth and help regain India's glorious legacy of development, while modernizing and renovating our precious heritage.

1

IMPERIALISM UPROOTS AGRICULTURE

India, by the prevailing standards of premodern times, i.e., until 1815, was the most prosperous nation in the world. Its trade with the world had flourished over several centuries prior to 1815, owing to India's ability to produce and trade what a large part of the world did not or could not produce till then, ranging from spices and textiles to medicines, agricultural implements, etc.

India had earlier enjoyed a massive balance of trade surplus with Europe, and with most other parts of the world. Merchants came from all over the world to purchase goods, unavailable or manufactured elsewhere, from Indian markets. In fact, it is widely believed that India was a low-cost producer of almost all consumer goods until the Industrial Revolution.

India's share of world income in AD 1700 was estimated at almost 25 per cent, about the same as that of the whole of Europe. It was higher (almost 50 per cent) prior to the Islamic invasion and disruption. By 1952, it dropped to less than 4 per cent share. India was also the global leader in cognitive sciences, for example, algebra, geometry, calculus, physics, chemistry, metallurgy, etc.

and the fundamental dimensions of mind development; i.e., what is known formally today as cognitive intelligence, and emotional, social, moral, spiritual, innovative and environmental intelligences, besides self-medical treatment via yoga (particularly pranayama) and Ayurveda.

However, things began to drastically change for the worse by the year 1815. This was an important turning point for two reasons—first, the defeat of the Maratha empire, which was led by Peshwa Baji Rao II, at the hands of the British imperialists, and second, the denial and blocking by British imperialists of science-based innovations such as locomotives and the Bessemer steel blast furnace, which were the engines of Industrial Revolution in Britain and later in Europe, till the late nineteenth century.

After the Rani of Jhansi-led First War of Independence (1857–58), the Indian economy witnessed a long, accelerated decline due to persistent British imperialist oppression, loot exported to England, and de-culturization through an imposed foreign-inspired education curriculum. This decline, from the mid-nineteenth century to 1947 (i.e., nine decades after 1857), transformed India from a prosperous, premodern developed country to a poor, underdeveloped modern nation by the standards of the twentieth century.

The constant bleeding of resources by British imperialists was first documented by Dadabhai Naoroji in 1869 in *Poverty and Un-British Rule in India*. Dr Utsa Patnaik and Dr Prabhat Patnaik, albeit Left-leaning Marxist economists, in their collection of essays titled *A Theory of Imperialism*[1] rebut the popular lore that the British as imperialists did not plunder India. Drawing on nearly two centuries of detailed data on tax and trade, the Patnaiks calculate that Britain drained nearly $45 trillion from

---

[1]Utsa Patnaik and Prabhat Patnaik, *A Theory of Imperialism,* Columbia University Press, 2016

India during the period 1765 to 1938. If a 'back of the envelope' calculation is further made for the period 1939–48, the total drain of Indian wealth to Britain would be $71 trillion. It is a staggering sum. For a perspective, $71 trillion is twenty-seven times more than the total annual GDP of Britain today.

This systematic loot happened through the rigged trade system, the zamindari revenue extraction mandate, and the collection made from taxes and levies imposed on Indians for British expenses incurred during World War I and II. Prior to the colonial period, Britain bought goods such as textiles, spices and rice from Indian producers and paid for them in the usual way—mostly with silver—as they did with any other country. But something changed in 1765, shortly after the East India Company took control of the subcontinent after the Battle of Plassey in 1757, and established a monopoly over Indian trade.

The modus operandi was as follows: The East India Company began collecting taxes in India, and then shrewdly used a portion of those revenues (about a third) to fund the purchase of Indian goods for British use. And then later, 'buying' from peasants and weavers, using money that had just been taken from them as land revenue by criminals appointed as 'zamindars' by the British Queen.

It was a theft on a grand scale. Yet, most Indians were (and are even today) unaware of the events of that period because the British officials collected the taxes, and the British business persons who showed up to buy their goods were not the same as the officials. 'Had it been the same person, they surely would have smelled a rat,' as British author Dr Jason Hickel of the University of London maintained in a recent article in *Al Jazeera*.[2]

---

[2]Jason Hickel, 'How Britain stole $45 trillion from India', *Al Jazeera*, 19 December 2018, accessed on 2 April 2019, https://www.aljazeera.com/indepth/opinion/britain-stole-45-trillion-india-181206124830851.html

To add to this, the British were able to sell the stolen goods to other countries at prices that were far higher than the cost at which these goods were 'bought' in the first place, pocketing not only 100 per cent of the original value of the goods but also the markup.

After the British Raj took over, the colonizers added a special new twist to the tax-and-buy system. As the East India Company's monopoly broke down, Indian producers were allowed to export their goods directly to other countries. But Britain made sure that the payments for those goods nonetheless ended up in London. This ensured that the British eventually had possession of all the gold and silver that should have gone directly to the Indians in exchange for their exports.

This exploitative system meant that even while India was running an impressive trade surplus with the rest of the world—a surplus that lasted for three decades in the early twentieth century—what showed up was deficit in the national accounts, because the real income from India's exports was being appropriated in its entirety by Britain. Moreover, as Dr Patnaik points out, '[The] cost of all Britain's wars of conquest outside Indian borders was charged always wholly or mainly to Indian revenues.'[3]

Thus, during the entire 200-year history of direct and indirect British rule in India, nationally and regionally, there was almost no increase in per capita income from 1870 to 1947. In fact, in the last three decades of the nineteenth century—the heyday of Britain's intervention—income in India collapsed by half. The average life expectancy of Indians dropped by one-fifth from 1870 to 1920. Tens of millions died needlessly due to seventeen *policy-induced famines* of the so-called British India government, whose direct rule excluded the princely states numbering then at

---

[3]Utsa Patnaik and Prabhat Patnaik, *A Theory of Imperialism*, Columbia University Press, 2016

600 (according to the Famine Commission Reports of 1890 and 1921). It is false to call British rule in India 'benign', as Indian Anglophile intellectuals did, and continue to even today. The truth is Britain did not develop India. Quite the contrary, it was India that developed Britain by financing the Industrial Revolution, the British administration and Britain's major wars. The British thus, siphoned out $71 trillion from a colonized and defenceless India till 1947.

Statistically, a macroeconomic view of India's rise and decline over the past 2,000 years was attempted in a systematic way by Dr Angus Maddison, a British economist, whose work on the subject, as of now, has received the widest acceptance. Recently, some Indian authors have updated his findings. Based on Maddison's data, India's per capita income from the year 1820 (in 1990 dollar terms) till 2010 is graphically shown below in Graph 1.

Graph 1
GDP Per Capita of India in 1990
International Dollars from 1820 to 2010

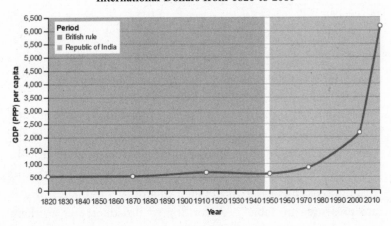

Source: S. Krishnamurthy, New York, USA; https://commons.wikimedia.org/wiki/File:GDP_per_capita_of_India_(1820_to_present).png

This chart is based on the research published by Maddison in 2001, with linear regression estimation of India's per capita income, and presented below (refer to Table 1).

Table 1

India's Relative Global Economic Position

India in	Per-capita GDP current prices	% of world population	% of world GDP
AD 1	$450	30.3%	32.0%
AD 1000	$450	27.2%	28.0%
AD 1500	$550	18.0%	24.4%
AD 1600	$550	18.0%	22.4%
AD 1700	$550	27.4%	24.4%
AD 1820	$533	20.1%	16.0%
AD 1870	$533	19.8%	12.1%
AD 1913	$673	16.6%	7.5%
AD 1950	$619	14.1%	4.2%
AD 1973	$853	15.1%	3.1%
AD 1998	$1,746	17.1%	4.1%
AD 2011	$4,636	17.3%	6.35%
AD 2017	$7,056	17.6%	7.3%

Source: Angus Maddison data; interpolated by Ripayan Chakraborty

Maddison's per capita income estimates for different periods for India, as shown in Table 1, highlight the fact that the growth in per capita GDP matches in declining proportion to population growth.

Recently, Stephen Broadberry, Johann Custodis and Bishnupriya Gupta (2015) updated Maddison's estimates, which are presented in Table 2. According to Broadberry et al, there was a significant decline in India's per capita income between 1600 and 1871, which includes the key period of Mughal rule (1600–1800), and for which we have data.

Table 2

PPP-adjusted Per Capita Income (PCI) (1990 International Dollars)

	Maddison	Broadberry/Bishnupriya et al
AD 1600	$550	$682
AD 1650	NA	$638
AD 1700	$550	$622
AD 1750	NA	$576
AD 1801	NA	$569
AD 1811	NA	$519
AD 1821	$533	$520
AD 1831	NA	$510
AD 1841	NA	$555
AD 1851	NA	$556
AD 1861	NA	$528
AD 1871	$533	$526
AD 1913	$673	NA
AD 1950	$619	NA

Source: Stephen Broadberry, Johann Custodis and Bishnupriya Gupta, 'India and the great divergence: An Anglo-Indian comparison of GDP per capita, 1600–1871', *Explorations in Economic History*, 2015, online. pp. 1–18

However, as measured by per capita income, this decline was briefly arrested between 1871 and 1913, when the British India government did allow some industrialists such as Tata to set up industries like steel, and some light industries by Birla, Godrej and others to counter rising European exports to India. But after World War I, this trend again became negative, as evidenced in my later research (see Table 3).

Table 3

PPP Per-Capita GDP

	India	UK	US
AD 1820	$533	$1,707	$1,257
AD 1870	$533	$3,191	$2,445
AD 1913	$673	$4,921	$5,301
AD 1950	$619	$6,907	$9,561
AD 1973	$853	$12,022	$16,689
AD 1998	$1,746	$23,491	$32,949
AD 2011	$4,636	$36,608	$49,794
AD 2017	$7,056	$43,877	$59,532

Source: Subramanian Swamy, 'The Response to Economic Challenge: A Comparative Economic History of China and India, 1870–1952', *The Quarterly Journal of Economics*, Vol No. 93(1), February 1979, pp. 25–46

The numbers above are in part drawn from Maddison (till 1998) and then updated for 2011 and 2017 using World Bank data.

Clearly, the year 1870 was an inflexion point of sorts for India's development under the British rule, when the Indian economy witnessed growth again after several centuries of decline. But this growth was much too slow compared to the rapid growth in the West (which was then in its phase of the Industrial Revolution, and in Britain, France, Portugal financed by extracted resources in large measure from India). While economic growth in India did resume in the industrial sector in the late nineteenth century, it is also true that the distance between India and the West had widened considerably by then.

This period is also significant because the internal rebellion and resistance in India to British imperial forces, which continued from 1757 to 1857, when the so-called 'Sepoy Mutiny' (known amongst Indians today as the 'Great Uprising' or the 'First War of Independence'), was crushed by British-led forces. In 1860, the Government of British India under Queen Victoria came into existence and from around 1870 began to formulate, directly or indirectly, policies for the Indian economy on a national basis.

One clear fact emerges: 1857 onwards, British imperialist outlook was one of complete distrust towards the Indian peasantry, which had supplied soldiers and also funded Rani of Jhansi and the Maratha revolt against direct and indirect British rule. After the Great Uprising of 1857, it became clear to the British that the peasantry, such as in the Rohilkhand and Oudh areas in the North, and Vellore in the South, had aided and financed the revolt against British rule. So grand was this support that Veer Savarkar wrote about it in his book *The Indian War of Independence 1857*. But sadly, this book is yet to be made required reading in schools and colleges.

In the aftermath of the events of 1857, the British India government under Queen Victoria launched a systematic assault on Indian farmers. The East India Company deliberately designed policies that bled agriculture of all its resources. In order to strengthen their political control on India, keeping the pressure on the peasants through an oppressive land revenue system seemed necessary to the colonial administration. The colonial government's decision to build such a feudal system for collecting land revenue was motivated by the political need to secure collaborators for imperial rule. In fact, an important reason for the decline in grain yield was such a policy of land revenue. The fall in per acre grain yield in India was mainly due to the sharp decline in rice and coarse-grain yields. Rice crop declined even in total output, at the rate of -0.09 per cent per year. However, the decline in the yield per acre in foodgrains in India did not commence from the mid-nineteenth century, but had begun earlier. The yield per acre in wheat and rice was 'very high' in the early nineteenth century and compared favourably with the yields obtained in 'scientific' agriculture in Europe. The decline in agricultural productivity, as measured by the yield per acre, began from 1750, and was prolonged and may have stretched for nearly two centuries, to 1950!

Notwithstanding the above assessment, agriculture suffered the most severe decline because of the revenue-extracting zamindari system set up by the British imperialists. The farmers were unable to pay the exploitative revenue to the British agents, who were referred to as zamindars. These zamindars were mostly criminals with unfettered power to collect revenue at will, provided a fixed amount was paid to the British government.

Since this government of foreigners needed a comprador local elite to govern securely, they encouraged the growth of an intermediary class that was obliged to deliver a fixed amount of revenue to the government. But this new class was fully empowered by the imperialists to extract what it pleased from the tenant cultivator and also keep the difference in amount for themselves. Thus, if a peasant in debt absconded or had died, the revenue collector (zamindar) had the power to demand from his neighbour to pay his debts on his behalf as well! This comprador class of moneylenders that rose in this process was under no compulsion to innovate for agricultural progress. They were absentees from the farm, and saw their role naturally as serving their English masters, from whom they drew their authority and received protection in return, and amassed wealth without contributing to productivity or taking any risks.

The character of the Indian colonial agricultural system thus was really feudal, not bureaucratic. Thus, the amounts that were collected as well as the machinery for realization were such that the indebtedness of the farmer, especially in grain cultivation, grew in an unprecedented way. The same view was expressed by the Famine Commission in its report in 1898:

> [Although the agricultural classes of India have not] at any
> known period of their history been generally free from
> debt...individuals and classes may have fallen into deeper
> embarrassment under the British Rule than was common
> under the Native dynasties which preceded it.[4]

In collecting land revenue, the government had to necessarily
assign responsibility of its payment and settlement on some
'self-dependable' persons. The choice the colonial government
made had a profoundly unsettling effect on the power structure
within the Indian society. Prior to the advent of the British, rent
was a collective responsibility of the panchayat, which was headed
by a patel (patidar), who also lived in the same village. This made
it necessary to evolve consensus and a willingness on the part
of the panchayat to share the economic setbacks of individual
peasants of the village.

The colonial land revenue system thus abolished this collective
responsibility of the panchayat and hence the social security in
villages as well. The new land tax was collected in money without
reference to a cadastral survey of productivity, paving the way
for the rise of the moneylender who would extend loans in his
individual capacity to the cultivator to enable him to pay the
fixed revenue. These assessments were excessive, and hence the
amount of land revenue grew 25 per cent between 1865 and
1900, and 21 per cent between 1900 and 1947 while the output
of grain had declined during this same period.

The colonial administration also introduced the modern
courts of law in urban towns to enforce the payment of loans

---

[4]Report of the Indian Famine Commission, 1898, accessed on 4 April 2019,
https://ia801701.us.archive.org/5/items/FamineCommissionReport/Famine%20
Commission%20Report.pdf

and taxes. The English system of courts wrested the judicial power of the panchayats, thereby empowering the moneylender even more, since he had a decided advantage in being able to process his court petitions with greater facility in urban towns against the peasant. Quick auctions of lands were arranged by the authorities, and soon, the moneylenders became the non-cultivating owners of land, first by ruining the peasant who had borrowed from him and then by pushing him further into debt. In each village of India, this basic pattern of change induced by the colonial land revenue system was common: the patels and the principal cultivators who had formerly guided the affairs of the village were reduced to the status of tenants tilling the fields of the moneylenders, and later became dispossessed.

Soon, a new class emerged in rural India dominated by the foreclosing creditor. More than two-thirds of the land came under tenants-in-cultivation, compared with only 30 per cent in feudal China. Rents paid by the tenants were generally 30 per cent higher than that paid by Chinese peasants, while the interest rates on loans were two to three times higher. Estimates of fifty years (1800–50) show that in the Varanasi district of Uttar Pradesh (UP), 40 per cent of the land had changed hands from the cultivator to the moneylender, although the ratio of agricultural debt to the value of agricultural land may have been no higher than 20 per cent and debt service to income about 5 per cent. Such was the rural oppression introduced by the British imperialists.

The aggregate land revenue collected by the government was sizeable despite the growing poverty and continued decline in agriculture. In the combined central and provincial budgets, the share of land revenue was 70 per cent in the early nineteenth century and about 36 per cent by the end of World War I. By 1946–47, the share of land revenue declined to only 7 per cent, but nevertheless, the absolute authority only impoverished the self-sufficient village communities, and completely disrupted the interdependence of groups within the village. As B.B. Chaudhuri states: 'It was the revenue measure of the government that proved the greatest depressor in the rural economy. Even the pervasive disaster (famines) did not make the government relent in the matter of revenue collection.'[5]

High land tax by itself does not obstruct agricultural development. Japan, under the reign of Emperor Meiji, had much higher taxes than India, but the mobilized resources returned to agricultural colleges and research stations, and in bettering agricultural techniques. This did not happen in India because of the naturally limited and negative role the British saw for themselves in the 'development' of India. Hence, under colonialism, there was a severe regression in the institutional framework of Indian agriculture.

The drain of Indian resources and wealth out of the country to England by British imperialists in the nineteenth century is amplified by a comparison of Indian economic history since 1870 with that of a similarly placed China. Both countries suffered at the hands of imperialism, but with a difference. China was never administratively controlled by foreigners. Throughout the period, it remained a country ruled by the Qing dynasty till 1911, after which the Chinese Revolution, in the same year, also called the Xinhai Revolution, led to the fall of the dynasty. Thereafter, Sun Yat-sen, leader of the Chinese Nationalist Party (Kuomintang), served as the first provisional president of the Republic of China (1911–12). He was succeeded by Chiang Kai-shek in 1925. Of course, the Chinese government was under constant threat of

---

[5]B.B. Chaudhuri, 'Rural Power Structure and Agricultural Productivity in Eastern India, 1757–1947', in *Agrarian Power and Agricultural Productivity in South Asia* (edited by Meghnad Desai, Susanne Hoeber Rudolph and Ashok Rudra), University of California Press, 1984, p. 138

destabilization and under siege from imperialist powers. India, on the other hand, had been defeated and subjugated by the British and administratively governed by men sent from Britain to rule India. The Indian government was thus a captive of foreigners in policymaking, with disastrous consequences.

The contrast between an imperialist-ruled India and a feudal China comes out clearly in the agricultural development of the two countries. Thus, although the yield per acre for all crops in China increased relative to India, the relative increase in output per se of China was much greater. This happened even though China was ruled by a feudal oligarchy during the entire period of 1870–1950, and had gone through political and military upheaval of the kind that India had not experienced; and yet, China's agricultural performance, especially in terms of grain output, was superior to India's in this period, as seen in tables 4 and 5.

Table 4
Long-term Growth Rate of Crops in China and India

(per cent per annum)

	China*	India
Output		
Foodgrains	+0.60	+0.11
Non-foodgrains	1.37	+1.31
Area		
Foodgrains	+0.49	+0.31
Non-foodgrains	+0.25	+0.42
Yield Per Acre		
Foodgrains	0.11	−0.20
Non-foodgrains	+1.12	+0.89

Population	0.60	0.67
Per Capita Output		
Foodgrains	+0.00	−0.56
Non-foodgrains	+0.77	+0.64

Source: For China: D.H. Perkins, *Agricultural Development in China, 1368–1968*, Aldine Publishing House, 1969. For India: George Blyn, *Agricultural Trends in India, 1871–1947*, University of Pennsylvania Press, 1966

*1871–1957, 1891–1947

Table 5
Ratio of Rice, Wheat and Cotton Yields
(China to India)

Crop	1921–25	1947
Wheat	1.20	1.50
Rice	1.52	3.29
Cotton	2.00	2.07

Source: 1921–25: J.L. Buck, *Chinese Farm Economy*, University of Chicago Press, 1930, p. 208; 1947: 'Economic Development in India and Communist China', Staff Study No. 6, Committee on Foreign Relations, U.S. Congress Washington D.C., 1956, p. 9

The contrast between the response of an indigenous government faced with a peasant-inspired rebellion, which is the case of China (after the Taiping Rebellion), and that of a colonial government in India after the 1857 Revolt, is, thus, striking. The native Chinese government responded by becoming more accommodating to the peasants, while the colonial foreign Indian government hardened in its approach towards peasants. This contrast in response also may be a reason why, during the whole period (1870–1950), China had only two major famines while India had twelve!

This contrast can also be seen more clearly in the growth experience of the directly British-ruled and the indirectly British-ruled Indian princely states. Table 6 summarizes the trend of grain output in these two regions of India, which shows that the states directly administered by the British performed much worse than the indirectly ruled princely states.

Table 6

Comparative Performance of British India
and the Princely States of India

	Units	Level 1940–41	Growth Rate (per cent/year) (1920–21 to 1940–41)
Foodgrain Output	**Million tons**		
British India		38.15	-0.35
Princely States		6.41	+1.52
Area under Foodgrains	**Million acres**		
British India		136.20	+0.25
Princely States		29.11	+0.18
Yield Per Acre	**Tons/acre**		
British India		0.28	-0.60
Princely States		0.22	+1.34
Population	**Millions**		
British India		295.81	+1.34
Princely States		93.20	+1.36

Source: Subramanian Swamy, 'Statistical Summary of the Social and Economic Trends in India (Inter War Period)', Office of the Economic Advisor, Government of India, New Delhi, 1945, pp. 6–9

From Table 6, we can infer that for the period for which data is available, namely 1920–21 to 1940–41, the states ruled by Indian princes as compared to British India experienced a faster growth in the output of grains and in the yield per acre, even though the area under cultivation grew faster in the latter area.

Because of this high growth rate in yield, the difference in the level of output per acre in foodgrains narrowed considerably to just 0.06 tons per acre. That is, while the per acre grain yield in 1940–41 in British-ruled India was 1.27 times the level in the princely states, in 1920–21, the yield per acre of grain in the former area was about double the yield in the latter. The reason for the initially much lower yield per acre in the princely states was that British India comprised the most fertile parts of India, while most of the princely ruled states had poor-quality lands or plain desert areas.

Interestingly, within British India, the wheat farmers of Punjab did not face the same hardships in land revenue. This is because in the late 1840s, after a series of wars, the Sikhs signed the Treaty of Lahore in 1846. One section of the Sikhs had sent soldiers to aid the British in crushing the rebellion of 1857 in Lucknow. Subsequently, the colonial government, as a political measure, enacted the Punjab Land Alienation Act of 1900 and the Rent Act to safeguard the rights of the peasant. Rents in Punjab, therefore, in sharp contrast to the rest of the country, could not be raised without a court order. Such an enactment for the rest of the country was vociferously demanded by the leaders of the freedom movement, but was denied by the British authorities on one pretext or another. This attitude of the colonial government towards Punjab is one of the most important reasons for the state becoming agriculturally better off than the rest of the country by the mid-twentieth century.

Other Dimensions

This contrast in performance between India and China also raises questions of technological as well as institutional issues. Data on irrigation, multiple cropping and the application of chemical fertilizers all indicate that China was more advanced than India in 1952. In China, 42 per cent more land was under irrigation, 22 per cent more land was under multiple cropping and 140 per cent more chemical fertilizers were being used per acre as compared to India. Further, irrigation and the application of fertilizers in India were diverted to cash crops marked for exports, as part of the British policy. The relatively higher level of agricultural technology in China that was achieved under much more difficult political circumstances, therefore, points to the stark negative role of the colonial Indian government in the nineteenth and the early twentieth centuries. This is further supported by the fact that in 1939–40, there was a small share of the area irrigated by government canals in the total irrigated area.

Clearly, the central reason why the grain yield per acre declined in India and not in China was due to the differing attitudes of the governments in the two countries. In China, the elite and the Qing dynasty were greatly sobered by the Taiping Rebellion, which was the most important political and religious upheaval in China in the nineteenth century. The ruling elite chose not to extract revenue through the land tax without considering the economic position of the peasant. The paochia and lichia indigenous systems kept good records of the peasant conditions, and through a system of granaries helped the peasant in bad times.

The government of India manned at the top by British nationals and the British government in London had two clear policy directions. First, that agriculture was to finance British India's treasury through confiscatory land revenue enabled by the zamindari system, and second to encourage the growth of cash crops on the best lands.

The need for cash crops by the British was influenced by certain international events. The American Civil War in 1864–65 led to the cessation of cotton supply to Britain, and hence the textile industry in Lancashire was in urgent need of cotton. India provided the alternative source, access to which became easier after the opening of the Suez Canal. This led to the switching of fertile lands to cotton cultivation. This aspect of the colonial policy hit the fertile rice areas, which were progressively switched to cash crops right up to the end of World War II. The then government's statistician, Mr S. Subramanian, states the following in his study:

> In spite of the best efforts on the part of the Agricultural Department in recent years to improve the quality and yield, the output of rice has obstinately (*sic*) refused to improve... had not the cash crops been comparatively more profitable it was a fair probability that the greater part of the increased area under irrigation would have been brought under rice cultivation.[6]

The colonial Indian government's policy of exporting cash crops, and the introduction of the railways from the principal port cities to the hinterland, increased incomes, which accrued to the apex of the rural power structure, such as the neo-landed moneylender class. However, this money was not invested in improved agricultural technology because of the aversion of this new absentee class to agricultural activities on the grounds of caste. Nor could it be channelled to industrial investment because, till World War II, the colonial government's policy was to restrict native Indian investment in modern industry. Therefore, the increased incomes either went into conspicuous consumption or into hoarding precious metals such as gold. Such attitudes are reflective of the uncertainties of the times, despite political stability

---

[6]Subramanian Swamy, 'Statistical Summary of the Social and Economic Trends in India (Inter War Period)', Office of the Economic Advisor, Government of India, New Delhi, 1945, pp. 6–9

in India. It is similar to the attitude of the Chinese peasant for a period in the post-1978 reform phase, when he diverted increased incomes to consumer durables, housing and hoarding rather than to agricultural investment.

By 1950, when India and China founded their new republics and commenced development through economic planning, China had a comfortable food surplus, which enabled it to finance rapid industrial growth. India, which had suffered a two-century-long decline in foodgrain yield, had no such cushion or surplus. Therefore, the unthinking imposition of the Soviet Union's model of planning led to a near-famine condition caused by a rain deficit in the 1960s. India was compelled to slow down its industrialization programme in the 1960s to provide resources for improvements in agriculture, after the realization dawned on free India's planners that the sector could not be squeezed any more without serious consequences for the economy as a whole.

2

INDUSTRIALIZATION: MISSED OPPORTUNITIES AND UNFULFILLED PROMISES

Unlike agriculture, the railways provide a counterexample of how the indigenous government in China, influenced by the conservative elite, could obstruct the introduction of modern technology. In 1881, almost thirty years after India had inducted the railways, Li Hsi-hung wrote to the Chinese emperor, stating 'eight reasons' why railroads in China would be 'infeasible' (e.g., it would lead to corruption of officials); 'eight reasons' why they would be 'unprofitable' (e.g., they would transfer goods from one province to another without increasing production); and 'nine reasons' why they would be 'harmful' (e.g., they would make it possible for foreigners to penetrate into the interiors). In 1876, a British company, Jardine Matheson and Company, laid the first tracks in Shanghai. This rail line connected British and American territorial settlements with the Wusong docks on the Huangpu River. But Shanghai's local governor quickly dismantled it, accusing the British of building the line without the permission

of the emperor in Beijing. It was only after signing the Treaty of
Shimonoseki in 1895[7] that the Chinese government was forced
to allow the development of railroads.

In contrast, there was no debate or doubt within India
regarding railways. Indeed, if there was any, it was in England
on the advisability of allowing railway construction in India on
the grounds that the railways could unite anti-imperialist forces.
The earliest offer to construct a railway line in India was made
in 1844 by Dwarkanath Tagore's mining firm, Carr, Tagore and
Company. This company offered to subscribe to one-third of
the capital required to build a railway line from the port city
of Calcutta (now Kolkata) north-west to the coalfields beyond
the town of Burdwan. The offer was not taken up. But with the
rising pressure exerted on London by English traders, especially
those who wanted to export cotton and opium (for sale in China)
from India, the British government finally agreed to enter into
negotiations with officials of the East India Company to form the
East Indian Railway (EIR). The terms offered were most attractive
in the then prevailing conditions of depression of 1848–49 in
England. The colonial Indian government agreed in 1848 to
ensure, for a period of ninety-nine years, a minimum return of
5 per cent on the invested capital by guaranteeing to pay the deficit
in the realized return. Further, land for laying the rails was free.
With these guarantees, the EIR had no difficulty in raising, in no
time, all but 1 per cent of the required capital in London itself.
As Cottrell[8] had noted, around this time, the British were under
pressure to find overseas outlets for their domestic savings, and
thus under the counter-guarantee agreement, the colonial Indian

---

[7]The peace treaty between Japan and China signed on 17 April 1895, which
concluded the first Sino-Japanese War (1894–95)
[8]P.L. Cottrell, *British Overseas Investment in the 19th Century*, Macmillan,
London, 1975, p. 11

government paid £15 million to cover the deficit in the rate of return (about 1.25 per cent).[9] Till 1900, the railway companies in India were in deficit, but thereafter, they were in a position to contribute to the government revenue. Till then, about 0.2 to 0.3 per cent of the national income was paid out to cover the deficit in the dividend to the English.

But the real impetus to the growth of railways came from two political events. The first was the Great Uprising of 1857, which convinced all doubting Thomases in London on the urgent need for railways. Most policymakers in Whitehall insisted that had the railways been there, the 1857 Revolt could have been put down more quickly. The second was the growing fear in the 1880s and 1890s about a possible Russian invasion via Afghanistan. This fear led to the British building railway networks in north-west India, which constituted a change of earlier policy. Up until then, the railway policy was merely to connect the ports of Bombay (now Mumbai), Calcutta and Madras (now Chennai) to hinterland markets to facilitate the export of cotton and jute.

Besides the British willingness, the Indians—unlike the Chinese—were ready for the railways too. As a consequence, India had acquired, by the time of Independence in 1947, the fourth-largest railway system in the world, for which the colonial government paid handsomely and fully. This advantage, despite the cost, placed India ahead of China in many areas of consequence. For example, although during the eight decades (1870–1950), India had twelve famines and China only two, the total deaths in this period ascribed to starvation due to famines in the two countries were the same, nearly 13 to 15 million. Similarly, after the founding of the two republics, China had a severe famine due

[9]Subramanian Swamy, 'The Response to Economic Challenge: A Comparative Economic History of China and India, 1870–1952', *The Quarterly Journal of Economics*, Vol No. 93(1), February 1979, pp 25–46

to drought in 1959–61, leading to deaths due to starvation (or induced by lack of food) to the extent of perhaps 32 million (in 1965–67, 1980 and 1987). India had the same intensity of drought, but no deaths due to those starvation incidents were reported by any national or international agency—due to the then superior rail and road transport, and a free press. That is, the lower per-famine death toll in India was in large measure due to the existence of the relatively larger railway network and, of course, free press. The Indian erstwhile advantage in the railways (and now no more), arising from a combination of British willingness to aid its cotton movement and troop deployment that began after the 1857 War of Independence, and Indian readiness to accept and pay the cost for it, is to be contrasted with the Chinese attitude.

Since railway construction in China had a long gestation lag, the Chinese till recently suffered from a weak transportation system. Since 2010, the Chinese government has invested heavily in railway infrastructure. The Traffic Intensity Ratio, measured as the ratio of the sum of tonne-kilometre of freight moved and passenger-kilometre to the GDP, even as late as 1981, was 4.0 in China and 5.1 in India, despite a rate of growth of freight and passenger traffic in China, which was double that of India's during 1952–81. It demonstrates that during these twenty-nine years, China had overloaded its railroad system. Following the Four Modernization programmes of Deng Xiaoping, this was rectified.

The railways in China did not promote economic growth because it was too small-scale. But, in India, although the railway network was extensive and relatively more developed, it failed to foster economic growth, because no structural changes in the economy resulted from its introduction. It addressed the British imperialist objectives of moving raw materials for British industry, such as cotton and metals, and British Indian troops.

The reason for the minimal impact of the railways on

the economic growth of the two countries was, in substance, the same. Both the Chinese and the Indian governments maintained the status quo in their attitudes, and were certainly fearful of the destabilization that could result from the railways. The Chinese government feared subversion by the outsider and suspected the railways would be the instrument for such activities. The colonial Indian government remained concerned by the potential for destabilization by the insiders, particularly the Indian entrepreneur, because of the non-parasitic economic power that would accrue from the railway facility. Yet, ironically, the railways were needed to keep that very same potential in check. The British resolved this dilemma by agreeing to the setting up of the railways, but making it difficult for any of its linkage benefits to reach Indian hands. Thus, the freight rates were designed to make internal trade less profitable than export. The access to railways measured by the fraction of per capita income that was required to be paid for the movement of 204 kilograms at a distance of 1,500 kilometres was 14 per cent in India, compared to only 0.6 per cent in the US and 1.3 per cent in Britain. Similarly, while it was demonstrated as early as 1865 in Bombay that locomotives could be produced in India (and these were supplied to the princely states), Britain insisted on exporting 12,000 locomotives to India during the period 1865–1941. This represented 22 per cent of the total British production. Even in labour requirements, until 1925, Britain insisted on India importing skilled personnel down to the platelayer or trackman for the railways. Nor did the Indian capital market benefit from the gilt-edged railway investment guarantee. London insisted until 1900 that the entire capital for the railways be raised in England. After that year, the responsibility for investment was vested in the government of India. Finally, the incentives to cotton exports and the easy import of textiles into the interiors made possible by the railways destroyed the Indian handicraft textile industry, rendering a large number of people unemployed. Most of all, the British India government ensured that the railway track gauge varied from broad gauge to medium gauge and narrow gauge. It was impossible those days to travel by rail from Delhi to Chennai without changing trains in an intermediate station.

Had the British *never* come, it is plausible that a government of Marathas led by the Peshwas would have imported the railway system from Britain commercially, as the rest of Europe did, and put India on the path of a development war with France and Germany. This counterfactual history, which needs to be debated, would have been largely positive for Indians on its own, but could not, because of the favourable circumstances in which the foreigner found himself in India. It has been less positive in China for much the same reason.

Judging by the estimates of growth of the manufacturing output for China derived by John K. Chang, and those assembled for India by Dr Morris D. Morris, a scholar of Economics from the US, the industrial growth rate of the two countries was nearly the same: about 5 per cent annually from World War I onwards. But by all important criteria, during the eight decades, 1870–1950, both China and India had failed to industrialize. The reasons for their failure were, however, quite different.

Both were victims of imperialism, but the content of imperialism was different in the two countries. In China, the Chinese government was besieged by five foreign governments— American and European—for concessions. Throughout the century (1850–1950), wars were waged by foreigners, and indemnity paid by China to foreign powers. Between 1842 and 1911, China paid indemnity 110 times. In the five years from 1895 to 1900, China made indemnity payments to Japan equal to twice the national receipts for the Ch'ing government in 1900.

In India, the British government ruled over native Indians, but there were, however, no wars, no combat and no serious disorder or rebellion after 1857 or until 1942. During the period 1870–1942, thus, there was stability, with no real challenge to the Government of British India. It is, therefore, significant that a Chinese government, functioning in disorder, war and rebellion, achieved almost the same growth rate in the manufacturing sector as the British government, which was operating in a remarkably stable environment with the tacit support of the literate sections of the population. This is significant because it is often asked why China was not able to utilize Western technology for economic advancement while Japan was able to. The question is often answered in terms of China's cultural narcissism, her arrogance and her introverted psychology. If this were indeed true, it would be difficult to explain why the government of India manned entirely at the top by the British was not able to achieve a rate of growth comparable to, at least, the Japanese level of 4 per cent per year in the early twentieth century. What blocked India from development? The answer to this is now obvious—imperialism.

It is significant that British investment in India was concentrated in the railways, in tea and coffee plantations, banks, mercantile establishments, and coal and jute mills. The notable omissions in the above list are cotton textiles, and iron and steel—the two industries that were largely instrumental in carrying out an epochal innovation in Britain's industrialization. Indians invested in these two industries later, but not without first having to overcome major hurdles placed by the British government of India. Sir Dinshaw Maneckji Petit, a Parsee entrepreneur, launched Oriental Spinning and Weaving Mill in 1855, the first-of-its-kind composite mill in Bombay, but it remained an isolated effort of a far-sighted individual. It was not until 1870 that the 'Government' of India began taking this threat posed by the modern textile industry, run and owned by Indians, seriously. In the steel industry, Jamsetji Tata, who pioneered the steel enterprise in India in the first decade of the twentieth century, had been blocked from launching any such project in the 1870s, despite being on the best of terms with the colonial Indian government. In fact, Tata had protested to David Lloyd George, the British prime minister during World War I, stating that this was an 'illustration of his contention that the industrial enterprise in India was often thwarted by official opposition'. The Tatas ultimately did succeed in setting up steel plants and producing steel at the lowest cost in the world (as seen in Table 1).

Table 1
Comparison of Work Costs: US and
Canada with TISCO (in 1923)

Cost	Canada (Tons/$)	US (Tons/$)	Jamshedpur (TISCO) (₹)	(Ton/$)
Pig Iron	**Million tons**			
Total materials' cost	24.70	24.00	36.12.0	12.27
Labour cost	0.85	1.00	2.11.0	0.89
Steel Ingots				
Total materials' cost	24.75	30.00	70.4.0	23.42
Labour cost	1.10	1.50	5.12.0	1.92
Blooms				
Materials	29.50	35.00	88.3.0	29.40
Labour	0.65	1.50	1.11.0	0.56
Rails				
Materials		41.00	123.0.0	41.00

Bars				
Materials	39.00	45.00	134.15.0	44.98
Labour	4.50		11.15.0	3.98

Source: ITB, Evidence by the Tata Iron and Steel Company (TISCO), Calcutta, 1924, op. cit., pp. 256–57. Quoted in S. Datta, 'Role of the Indian Worker in Early Phase of Industrialization', Economic & Political Weekly, XX, No. 48, 30 November 1985

Note: TISCO mentions that 'cost of pig iron at the blast furnace does not agree with the price charged to ingots in United States of America and Canada as they use an average price when charging to the open hearth furnaces.'

Examples of other industries such as jute and tea point to a similar hardening of attitude by the British-ruled government to native Indian entrepreneurship. It was only after 1870 that the need to industrialize received widespread acceptance by Indians. Around this time, India was institutionally ready for modern economic growth, if the government of the day had wanted it. If it had, our economic history would have been entirely different and free of poverty today. So why did the government resist native initiative in these areas? Why were British investments confined to export and export-related activities? The answer is obvious, and its impact is clear. India was made to miss the bus and has been running behind ever since to catch it.

The hypothesis, which has considerable support in evidence, may thus be expressed as follows. The slow industrialization in India in the nineteenth and early twentieth centuries cannot be attributed to the lack of native entrepreneurship, insufficient size of the market or the non-existence of acceptable rates of return. It can, on the other hand, be ascribed to the British India government for placing obstacles in the path of indigenous investment, and failing to provide economic leadership.

The goal of economic growth was never formulated by the British-run government until power was transferred to Indian hands in 1947. On the other hand, native business groups such as the Tatas, engineers such as Sir M. Visvesvaraya, and political leaders such as Dadabhai Naoroji, Bal Gangadhar Tilak and later Mahatma Gandhi were fully seized by the need for industrialization from their own special perspectives. It was the combination of British interests and the underlying social ethos of the government of India that they were here 'to govern, to stabilize, and to administer', but not to transform. This proved to be the main cause of India's slow development and disadvantaged position it found itself in, in 1952. Both James Mill and his eminent son John Stuart Mill took the utilitarian view that providing the government with the infrastructure to 'govern' the 'defective Hindu' was an end in itself. John Stuart Mill, in fact, stated: 'The question is, in what manner Great Britain can best provide for the government, not of three or four millions of English colonists, but of 150 million Asiatics who cannot be trusted to govern themselves.'

The few estimates that we can find on the government of India's public investment allocation highlight this exclusive concern 'to govern' to the exclusion of other development activity. Of the total gross expenditure of the government of India, defence accounted for 40 per cent, averaging about 3 per cent of the national income. The allocation for defence, however, constantly increased between 1870 and the 1940s, reaching 7.7 per cent of the national income in 1944. Significantly, in post-Independence budgets, defence expenditure has been generally less than 3 per cent of the national income. The large and increasing expenditure for defence was, however, only partly due to the British concern to contain internal uprising. Other reasons were that the government of India and Britain were concerned about a Russian invasion of India, especially during the late nineteenth and early twentieth centuries. Britain also sent Indian troops to China, Persia (now Iran) and Africa (and to the World Wars) as part of its imperial adventures. In World War I, nearly a million Indian soldiers were deployed abroad (among them was Gandhi, before he became the Mahatma).

In 1917, India's defence budget in current prices was £30 million, or almost twice the amount, forty years later, in 1957. Only 12 per cent of this outlay was on capital items. The government of India paid not only for the rising recruitment of Indian soldiers, but also for the British officers and soldiers who led them. Under the decree issued after the Great Uprising of 1857, it was stipulated that no Indian could hold a commissioned rank in the army, and that for every three Indian soldiers, there had to be one British officer or soldier. This was the policy till World War II.

Thus, India's contact with foreigners or the West was at best a missed opportunity and at the most that of an unfulfilled promise of the development of India using the innovations of the Industrial Revolution in Europe and the US. But, it is my conclusion that India got the worst of the possibilities. This was because the role of the colonial government was obstructionist, and blocked the proper transfer of technology. In fact, the social movements of Raja Ram Mohan Roy, Swami Dayanand Saraswati and Mahadev Govind Ranade could have laid the foundation for a fruitful collaboration between Britain and India, much like the one that developed between Meiji Japan and the United States in the nineteenth century. But, instead, the British chose to become increasingly racist and exploitative in India, the foundation for which was laid in Macaulay's *Minute on Education*, which was presented to the British Parliament in 1833. Macaulay debunked India's developed past, not only in the economic sphere but also in science, mathematics and spiritual advances. Instead, Macaulay derisively commented in the British Parliament that one shelf of a British library was superior to the entire literature in Sanskrit, and therefore ordered the banning of Sanskrit-medium schools and universities (i.e. gurukulas or gurukulams) and instead encouraged teaching of English and British etiquette.

This racism then led to a national awakening and the revolt of 1857, and then to increasing rebellion and confrontation evoked by the teachings of Swami Vivekananda, followed by the writings of Dadabhai Naoroji, Sri Aurobindo, Subramania Bharati and, finally, Mahatma Gandhi, among others, which led to freedom and liberation in 1947 after ninety years of struggle.

An interesting question that arises from the above analysis is about the level of development, in comparative terms, that China and India had reached in the late 1940s after nearly a century of confrontation with foreigners. Specifically, did China and India start their respective modern post-war economic planning as free nations from the same or similar outcome in levels of development?

Many general similarities existed between the economies of India and China at the time India achieved Independence in 1947 and the communists assumed power in China in 1949. Each had made modest beginnings towards industrialization. The existing modern factories in both countries were devoted to the production of light consumer articles, particularly textiles. Though the Japanese had developed heavy industry during their occupation of Manchuria in China, they were not integrated with the Chinese economy until later and after much of the equipment had been removed by the Russians after World War II. China and India began their development programmes, therefore, from a point at which neither country had made any great progress in capital-intensive large and heavy industry. In each country, a large percentage of the industrial production came from cottage and handicraft industries. In adjudging the industrial development of China as of 1949, American economist and political theorist

Walt Whitman Rostow in his *Stages of Economic Growth* opus placed it on a par with that of post-war India and with Japan in 1920–25, Russia in 1913, and the United States in 1870.

In addition, the new government in both China and India had to cope with extraordinary economic dislocations. In India, these dislocations resulted from the Partition of the subcontinent by the British, as a parting kick in 1947, to create Pakistan at the time of Independence. Our food position had been serious since the Burma Rice Bowl was separated from India in 1937. Food had been imported since about 1943. As a result of the Partition, India retained about 82 per cent of the population, received only 69 per cent of the irrigated area, 65 per cent of the wheat area and 68 per cent of the rice area. As a result of communal disturbances in Punjab in the late summer of 1947, some five million Hindu refugees had crossed into India from the newly formed Pakistan. Therefore, the government of India was faced with the task of feeding and housing the millions of uprooted refugees. West Punjab, Sind and the Sylhet district of Assam, which annually produced nearly a million tons of surplus grain, became part of Pakistan. India's textile industry was disrupted as a result of the inclusion of extensive jute- and cotton-producing areas in Pakistan, even as the textile mills remained in India. Our industrial production, which had expanded during World War II, had declined in the immediate post-war period. Reconversion to peacetime production had been slow. Machinery was worn out and outdated. The replacement of lost capital equipment during World War II (1939–45) was difficult.

The relative position of China and India just prior to the launching of their economic development programmes is reflected in Table 2.

Table 2
Level of Key Indicators: China and India
(around the time of founding of the republic)

	Indicator	Unit	Year	China	India	Ratio
1	Per Capita	1970 Parity$	1952	101	154	0.66
2	Population	millions	1952	574.8	367.0	1.57
3	Birth Rates	per 000	1950	37.0	40.0	0.93
4	Death Rates	per 000	1950	18.0	28.0	0.64
5	Life Expectancy	years	1950	40.0	32.0	1.25
6	Infant Mortality	per 000 births	1950	175.5	190.0	0.92
7	Adult Illiteracy	per cent	1950	25.0	20.0	1.25
8	Calories	per capita	1952	1917.0	1540.0	1.24
9	Foodgrains	mill.tons	1952	163.9	69.9	2.35
10	Yield	tons/hectare (ha)	1931–37			
		Rice		2.5	1.3	1.90
		Wheat		1.0	0.6	1.56
11	Sugar	tons	1952	0.5	1.8	0.25
12	Irrigation	per cent	1949	20.7	14.6	1.42
13	Cropping	Index	1949	135.4	111.1	1.22
14	Ammonium Sulphate	000 tons	1951	129.0	53.7	2.40
15	Steel	mill. tons	1952	1.4	1.1	1.25
16	Cotton Textiles	million Spindles	1956	7.2	12.4	0.58
		000 Looms	1956	115.0	207.0	0.56
17	Coal	mill. tons	1952	66.0	39.3	1.68
18	Electric Power	billion kilowatt hour (kWh)	1952	7.3	6.1	1.20
19	Crude Oil	mill. tons	1952	0.4	0.4	1.01
20	Cement	mill. tons	1952	2.9	4.1	0.71
21	Railways	000 km	1950	25.7	54.8	0.47
22	Highways	000 km	1949	130.2	391.8	0.33

23	Literacy	per cent	1951	14.3	16.7	0.86
24	Students Enrolled in Higher Education	(000s)	1954	253.0	594.1	0.43
25	College Graduates	(000s)	1952	32.6	72.1	0.45
	Percentage in Technological Subjects			31.4	17.8	

Source: Data culled from official statistical abstracts of the two countries. For China, the primary sources are publications of the State Bureau, Beijing, the World Bank, and James Tsao: 'China's Economic Development Strategies and their Effects on U.S. Trade', USITC Publication No. 1645, February 1985, Washington D.C. For India, we have relied on basic statistics relating to the Indian Economy, Centre for Monitoring Indian Economy (CMIE), Bombay, August 1984.
Note: The grain yield figures for India are different for the period 1936–39.

From Table 2, we see that just prior to the two countries embarking on planned economic development, China was ahead of India in per capita output terms, in foodgrains, agricultural inputs (such as irrigation, double cropping and fertilizers), and in coal since the China-India output ratio for these commodities exceeded the population ratio. The fact that the population ratio of 1.57 exceeded the output ratio for all others implied that India was ahead of China in per capita terms of these other commodities.

China was also ahead of India in terms of per capita calorie value of consumption and this is reflected in a better level of food output and health, which is measured by lower death rates and higher life expectancy. In other words, at the advent of planned economic development, China was better fed and healthier, relative to India.

But India was ahead of China in the early 1950s in several commodities of industry. India was also leading in per capita production of light industry, such as cotton textiles and sugar. India was clearly ahead in railways and highways, and it definitely had a superior industrial and transportation infrastructure (but not any more). Although literacy rates were higher in India in 1951, the percentage of college graduates holding degrees in technological subjects was more in China.

If we were to generalize on the basis of these ratios, we can say the following: (i) that at the dawn of planned economic development in 1952, China was clearly ahead of India in agriculture. This was, however, not so in 1870 when China and India were on a par. In other words, relative to India, China made much greater progress in agriculture during the period 1870–1952. (ii) India had, however, gone ahead in industry and transportation, as a consequence of which the country's per capita income in 1952 *was about 54 per cent higher than China's* in the same year.

In 1870, both countries were, however, on a par, and the varying internal stability and the differential impact of the West on these two countries produced that kind of structural divergence by 1952. The positions so described represent the initial conditions for the subsequent industrialization of India.

There is, at present, no acceptable theory as to which set of initial conditions is better for industrialization of a low per capita-income country, but it is clear that China in the early '50s was better placed than India for the Soviet Model of Planning, i.e., for extracting resources from agriculture to finance the Five-Year Plans' industrialization programme. Hence, the heavy industry-oriented socialist strategy made more sense for Chinese planning than for India, which, relative to China, required it to pay more attention to agriculture on a priority. India did not implement this strategy and slavishly adopted the Soviet-style planning until the food crisis of 1966–67, and the 1973 nationalism of wholesale trade.

But surprisingly, despite the total political stability in India, and the lack of it in China due to ideological disruptions, such as of the Great Leap Forward of 1957–59, the growth rate in per capita income over these eight decades was about the same, averaging an annual growth rate of 0.5 per cent to 0.6 per cent. This level, while by no means negative, was low by the standards of those countries which industrialized during the late eighteenth and early nineteenth centuries, and was considerably lower than the rates achieved by China and India, post 1980, when both nations began to dismantle, dilute or amend the Soviet model.

The colonial Indian government's tax policy towards agriculture was exploitative to the extent of causing a decline in the yield per acre of foodgrains, and thus lowering the level of living. Chinese agriculture experienced no such decline, as a consequence of which the per capita grain output, which was on a par with India in 1870, increased over the eight-decade period to reach 2.4 times the level in India in 1952. This crucial finding suggests that India stood at a disadvantaged position as compared to China in its initial conditions for pushing industrialization. There was thus simply no scope for squeezing agriculture to even fractionally finance industrialization. On the contrary, the initial conditions were such that agriculture should have been given first priority in economic planning in free India. The failure of Indian planners to recognize this fact has proved to be a major policy blunder that has been a drag on India's progress since 1952, and the blame rests squarely with Prime Minister Jawaharlal Nehru and his advisors with limited knowledge of Economics, such as P.C. Mahalanobis, whose approach to economic policy was bereft of reality. There is a lesson in this even today for Prime Minister Modi and his advisors.

Although the colonial government in India introduced and developed a railway network to promote foreign trade and further its control over the Indian masses, this network did not foster economic growth because of the colonial government's railway policy on line location, the varying gauge incompatibility and freight rates. Nevertheless, the existence of this confounding railway network prevented the occurrence of a famine in 1966–67 in India—the kind that had caused 32 million deaths due to starvation and consequent diseases in China under similar circumstances (in 1959–61).

The conclusion that emerges from a comparative analysis of these two Asian giants is that it is the absence of good leadership in the area where it would have been the most effective—in the government—that appears to explain the failure by the two countries to industrialize. Both countries were governed by unpopular governments that emerged neither out of a revolution of the masses nor out of a vote in democracy. Both governments were afraid of development and social change, and moved in that direction only when threatened. This is further confirmed by the fact that after liberation in the late '40s, when China and India had new but popular governments, both countries developed much faster than before. There is thus no substitute for a strong, enlightened government.

In a nutshell, therefore, China was relatively much better positioned to embark on industrialization in 1952 than India because its agriculture was not in a shambles as India's in 1947. Although India had a relatively better infrastructure than China, the difference was not much.

Hence, it was a monumental error for India later to have pushed for industrialization in a socialist Soviet model, without first having laid the foundation for agriculture. It is for this reason that the Indian regression relative to the West continued even after Independence. As late as 1998, the relative gap between the US and Indian per capita incomes was far greater than the gap in 1950. This regression in agriculture, in part, explains our disillusionment with the Left-leaning socialist, economic policies advocated and pursued after Independence, first by Pandit Nehru and later by his Congress party successors, especially his daughter, Indira Gandhi, and grandson, Rajiv Gandhi.

While it is true that even the 'Nehruvian' growth rates were arguably higher than the growth rates at any point in the pre-1947 five hundred years, they were totally out of step with the pace that was being set in the developed world or available opportunities in post-Independent India. The relatively contemporary poor performance had to do with the economic policies that was tutored by the pro-Soviet Union and its mentally captive Indian intellectuals, and the arbitrary restrictions placed on domestic economic activity based on licenses and quotas. This led to the growth of black markets, corruption and consequently inefficiency in this use of resources. The nation's growth rate in GDP, thus was, stagnant at around 3.5 per cent per year for forty years (1950–90). This was a huge lost opportunity available after Independence in 1947.

3

THE ALBATROSS AROUND INDIA'S ECONOMIC NECK: THE SOVIET MODEL

India's economic journey from an impoverished and underdeveloped country in 1947 to a developing nation in 1990 and thereafter to an emerging global economy from 1991 onwards, while protecting its gigantic democracy, serves as a remarkable example for other developing nations of the world. To better understand this economic voyage, I have, in this book, divided the period from 1947 till the introduction of reforms in 1991 and thereafter, in three distinct phases: (i) 1947–80, (ii) 1980–90 and (iii) 1991 till date.

Phase 1, from Independence in 1947 till 1980, underlines the highs and lows of the Nehruvian model of centralized economic planning borrowed from the Soviet Union. During this crucial period, India more or less followed a closed Soviet model in which the core was the concept of 'command economy', which envisaged a dominant role for the government in economic decision-making and strict adherence to import substitution as a policy, with the implied debunking of the theory of comparative advantage in foreign trade.

Phase 2 traces the opening up of the command, international trade economy during the decade from 1980–90. This phase was characterized by permitting Indian industries short-term foreign capital loans from private sources abroad and foreign collaboration in selective technology. Special schemes were also drawn up for attracting foreign funds and deposits from non-resident Indians (NRIs). The mismatch was accentuated by the use of the short-term foreign loans for long-term gestation projects in India, since the short-term loans became due for repayment in 1990, while the latter generated revenue (for repayment of the foreign loans taken) only after ten to fifteen years. This period mismatch caused a foreign exchange crunch because there were insufficient foreign exchange reserves, resulting in a crisis in 1990—a crisis I had to deal with as a senior Cabinet minister and a member of the Cabinet Committee on Political Affairs (CCPA). The Chandra Shekhar government came on the verge of a default of payment of debt due to foreign entities giving the 1985–88 short-term loans.

The context was ironic for the command economy of India. The rise of communism in Russia in the second decade of the twentieth century led to the emergence of the USSR. In the 1930s, carefully doctored reports released by the Soviet Politburo lauded the achievements of the Soviet command economy, and its instruments of economic planning. These reports generally were surprisingly and incredulously accepted. It had a profound intellectual impact, particularly on the siblings of India's nouveau riche, including people like Kim Philby and Donald Maclean in Britain who were later declared as spies of the Soviet Union. These India's children of the 'comprador' class were created by the land revenue-collection establishment—children who had gone to England as students to get 'Oxbridge' degrees and then entered the bureaucracy through the civil service examinations. A section of the academia in England was already under the influence of the Left movement sponsored by the Soviet Union, which, in the mid-1930s, vehemently supported India's Independence struggle, because it was anti-imperialist to do so.

This movement attracted Indian students. In fact, most of the Indian students who got recruited into the Left movement in Britain were from the rich landowning and comprador class. But there was a vested interest in conjunction with this intellectual commitment. A Soviet-type socialist economy meant land reform and usurpation by the state. But paradoxically, it meant no loss of power over marshalling the resources of the economy. This future elite's control over the state by virtue of its privileged education meant strategic placement and positioning in a future independent government of India. By the interlocking of families through marriages, caste brotherhood and cronyism, they ensured not only that, but they were also able to see to it that anyone who did not accept this socialist oligarchic dogma in Indian society found it difficult to secure any position of authority or even any employment. Thus, the future policymakers and elite of to-be-Independent India became easy targets for the Left, and an overwhelming number became adherents of the Leftist ideology as well. For them, state-directed economic planning became an article of faith.

Till the collapse of the USSR in 1991, this power structure remained firmly in place in India, and this explains much of India's dependence on the Soviet Union's ideology till then, even in the international affairs of India.

This USSR-inspired economic strategy was foisted on the Indian people in the '50s by Nehru—surprisingly without much debate. This was not the strategy that Mahatma Gandhi or Sardar Patel had advocated during the freedom struggle. The author of this strategy, namely Nehru, wanted the Soviet model adopted for reasons connected with his friendship with Lord and Edwina Mountbatten, but paradoxically, this Left ideology suited the interests of two powerful vested groups within our country: the feudal comprador class and the Left-inspired Indian intellectuals called the 'Kim Philby' group. The latter group gave Nehru the necessary intellectual baggage and they used their friendship with him to secure posts in key positions in the government, press, and academic and diplomatic services after India achieved Independence in 1947.

This feudal class, deprived of its lands under the post-Independence abolition of zamindari system, found that under this model, it continued to enjoy patronage power in the socialist Indian economy. It was this firm grip on the decision-making apparatus of the state that subsequently, after India's Independence, made the ideology of the likes of Gandhi and Patel irrelevant at the political level, and also sought to relegate a personality like C. Rajagopalachari to the status of an American-inspired crank. There was little challenge elsewhere in the country after Gandhi's assassination in 1948 and Patel's death in 1950.

Amongst the political leaders of the '50s and '60s, it was only Charan Singh who had dared to question the appropriateness of the Soviet model. But he, too, could not make much headway because of the intellectual hostility of the Left-feudal combine. In fact, despite Charan Singh being one of the most well-read political stalwarts and a prolific writer on Economics, he was dismissed in the media as a semi-literate 'kulak'[10], whose ideas were a mere rehash of Adam Smith's *laissez faire* (free enterprise).

There was thus a reassuring feeling among the vested interest groups that economic planning would merely transfer power to

---

[10]A communist term which means 'landlord'

them as civil servants and elite politicians, and dispose resources from the right hand to the left. That is why the Left-leaning siblings of zamindars and the comprador class found no intellectual difficulty in adjusting to the 'socialist pattern' of Indian society. This confluence of intellectual commitment to command economy and vested interests to maintain control over resources laid the secure foundation of the new Indian state's resolve to usher in economic planning in the Soviet framework.

The Soviet command economy model was formally adopted in the Second Five-Year Plan (1956–61). It envisaged an investment strategy of delaying consumption and investing the additional savings in the capital-intensive sector (loosely termed 'heavy industry'), and also by extracting surpluses of the agricultural sector to finance the industrialization programme. It was also presumed that demand for capital goods would be adequate and created by its own supply!

The grafting of this model on Indian planning was done by a physicist-turned-statistician who had little or no formal education in Economics—Professor P.C. Mahalanobis, founder of the Indian Statistical Institute (ISI), Calcutta. Mahalanobis, a confirmed Left intellectual, had plagiarized a Soviet growth model of the 1920s authored by Grigory Feldman, and introduced it into Indian planning without acknowledging the original authorship. For years, Feldman's model was passed off in India as 'Mahalanobis' Growth Model', till Massachusetts Institute of Technology (MIT) Economics Professor Evsey Domar discovered his plagiarism from his book *Essays in the Theory of Economic Growth*[11], and laid it bare. Just as Feldman's model failed in the USSR, it was a disaster in India as well, since the model's basic assumption of prosperous agriculture providing funds for industrialization was impossible

---

[11]Evsey Domar, *Essays in the Theory of Economic Growth*, Oxford University Press, 1958

in India especially since agriculture had been bled dry by the British imperialists.

In addition to the premise that agriculture would be in a position to provide funds for industrial growth, there were two other untenable assumptions that ensured that the model was wholly unsuited to Indian economic conditions. Firstly, that consumption could be postponed for an extended period and even curtailed; and secondly, that supply of capital goods would generate its own demand for it.

In 1947, as India became free, the nation had just emerged from a terrible famine in Bengal, a long freedom struggle and a bloody Partition, not to mention a World War that had depleted its meagre resources. The large masses of rural India were either at the poverty line or below it. There was very little scope to tighten its belt. On the contrary, a steady increase in wage goods was necessary to raise the standards of living. As noted earlier, agriculture had been bled to subsistence levels by the constant appropriations exacted by the British Indian colonial-landlord setup. The sector itself was in dire need of resources, if it was not to slide down any further. Clearly, agriculture was in no position thus to finance industrialization.

The speed and efficiency with which the independent government of India was able to set up the planning process was because the consensus for economic planning was shaped over decades prior to Independence, made possible in an otherwise culturally and religiously individualistic society by the confluence of two powerful interests referred to above. This consensus was made because of the intellectual ferment caused by controlled media news of the successes of Soviet planning.

The genesis of the planning process could be traced to the publication of *Planned Economy for India* by the distinguished

engineer-administrator M. Visvesvaraya, in 1934.[12] It was not
in any sense a comprehensive or theoretical exposition on
planning. The book, however, contained a clear statement of
objectives and targets and the methods to achieve them over
a period of five to ten years. Visvesvaraya was no Leftist, but
a nationalist moved by the consensus that was being skilfully
shaped. He listed 'Ten Urgent Requirements' for the economy,
including elementary mass education and training in defence.
Priority was accorded to industrialization: a six-fold increase
in the value of the annual industrial output, the output of iron
and steel to increase from 1.6 million tons to 3 million tons in
five years, and the output of coal to increase from 24 million
tons to 40 million tons over the same five years. Visvesvaraya
envisaged the establishment of the automobile industry and the
manufacture of 20,000 vehicles a year. The plan for agriculture
was modest, the net value of agricultural output was expected
to increase by 25 per cent in ten years. He also provided targets
for transport, railways, roads, shipping and communications. On
the basis of these physical targets, Visvesvaraya calculated an
expected increase in employment in the organized industry from
1.5 million to 10 million and for workers in all industries from
15.4 million to 50 million within five years. He envisaged a decline
in the numbers supported by agriculture. His plans provided for
an increase in educational facilities, both at the school and the
university levels, mass literacy to increase from 8 per cent of the
population to 50 per cent in ten years. The total cost of ₹10 crore
per annum (1934 prices), envisaged by him as the required plan
outlay, was to be met by the Central government (₹2 crore)
and provinces (₹8 crore). The capital expenditure required by
heavy industry, public works, public utilities and transport was

---

[12]M. Visvesvaraya, *Planned Economy for India*, Bangalore Press, 1934

to be financed partly with local loans and partly from profits of industries and agriculture, and to some extent from foreign loans. Whatever may have been the practicality and workability of the plan, Visvesvaraya fired the imagination of the educated class.

The idea of economic planning received further impetus when the Indian National Congress (INC) formed Congress governments in several provinces in 1937. An interprovincial committee was formed to consider 'urgent and vital problems, the solution of which was necessary for a scheme of national reconstruction and planning'[13]. In October 1938, a conference of the ministers of industries of the Congress-ruled provinces met and passed a resolution '...that problems of poverty and unemployment, of national defence and of the economic regeneration in general cannot be solved without industrialization. As a step towards such industrialization, a comprehensive scheme of national planning should be formulated'[14]. They recommended immediate steps to set up large-scale industries for producing machine tools, electric plants and accessories, heavy chemicals and fertilizers, and power-generation equipment, which were conspicuous by their absence in India. On the suggestion of the then Congress President Subhash Chandra Bose, the National Planning Committee (NPC) was set up in 1938, under the chairmanship of Pandit Nehru, and consisted of 350 members, including stalwarts such as Visvesvaraya and noted economist, K.T. Shah. The NPC was divided into twenty-nine separate subcommittees, each dealing with a separate and specific problem area. It held several meetings between June 1939 and September 1940. Later, due to the outbreak of World War II, the resignation of the Congress

---

[13]Brief notes on National Planning Committee of India, accessed on 28 June 2019, http://www.preservearticles.com/economics/brief-notes-on-national-planning-committee-of-india/7615
[14]Ibid.

governments in provinces, and the arrest and imprisonment of several of its members, the NPC could not function at the anticipated pace. It resumed work in 1946, after the end of the war. In spite of its functioning under handicaps, the NPC came out with a development perspective for the Indian economy.

The NPC's perspective plan stipulated a 200–300 per cent increase in the national income within a period of ten years; provision of basic minimum needs; provision of proteins, carbohydrates and minerals with 2,400–2,800 calories for an adult worker; ensuring availability of thirty yards of clothing per year and providing housing to the extent of at least 100 square feet per capita. As regards forms of national wealth, agricultural land, mines, quarries, rivers and forests, it was maintained that the ownership 'must absolutely be with the people of India' (i.e., nationalized). Cooperative farming was to be encouraged, and the zamindari was to be ended and ownership of land given to the tiller. On the question of nationalization of industries, there was a general agreement that small-scale and consumer goods industries should be in the private sector, though under strict government regulation and control, 'to conform to the national interest'. With regard to key industries, while the majority of members were in favour of state ownership, the minority thought that state 'control' would be sufficient. Some members of the NPC, including Pandit Nehru, recommended nationalization of banks and insurance companies, and state participation in foreign trade, especially in the case of essential commodities. The recommendations of the NPC did not constitute a development plan, but its publication and deliberations created a consciousness for the need for economic planning as a solution to the problems of underdevelopment and deteriorating economic conditions.

In 1944, another Plan that received great public attention was the Bombay Plan, also called the 'Big Business Plan', since it was published with the signatures of well-known, big businessmen, including J.R.D. Tata and G.D. Birla. It called for tripling the per capita GDP by doubling productivity of agriculture and increasing the output in the industrial sector by approximately five times in the above time frame. The Plan provided for a total outlay of ₹10,000 crore, allocated amongst several sectors: about 45 per cent for industry and 12 per cent for agriculture. The major sources for plan resources were the 'unearthing of hoarded wealth', sterling assets, surplus in balance of trade, foreign borrowing and deficit financing. Cooperative farming was proposed to replace landlordism with compensation to landlords. A strong plea was made for a more equal distribution of income through various policies, including provision of essential social services such as education and health, subsidies for utility services and progressive direct taxes, limiting profits through fixed prices and fixing minimum wages in certain well-established large-scale industries. The Bombay Plan called for growth of the public sector in the establishment of the basic and heavy large-scale industries and provision of economic and social infrastructure. The consumer goods industry, however, was to continue to function in the private sector.

Though the Bombay Plan was authored by noted businessmen, it leaned towards socialist planning. Such was the atmosphere! It generated a sharp controversy, since the socialists were not satisfied. They found the Bombay Plan's approach of gradual control of only the basic and key industries, with the rest of the industries in the private sector, unacceptable. They countered the Plan with a 'People's Plan' of M.N. Roy (a Soviet-trained intellectual who was later disowned by them), which articulated the view that production must be so organized as to eliminate the profit motive. In agriculture, land was to be nationalized and rural indebtedness abolished. The Plan proposed to de-emphasize cottage industries and gradually shift the resources to large-scale industries. The finances for the Plan would be found through direct taxation, diversion of the surplus profits to the state, and export of surplus agricultural products. The People's Plan obviously incorporated the strategy of Soviet planning in toto.

Naturally, in the debate that ensued, the priority accorded to large-scale industries came in for criticism from the disciples of Mahatma Gandhi, who believed the key to the solution of poverty and unemployment lay in the development of cottage industries in decentralized and independent village communities.

In view of the popularity of the concept of planning, the British government in India created a Board of Industrial and Scientific Research in 1940, followed by the appointment of a Reconstruction Committee of the Viceroy's Council. These organizations were given the task of preparing schemes for industrial development and research to be undertaken after World War II. In June 1944, a Planning and Development Department was established under Sir Ardeshir Dalal, who had also been associated with the Bombay Plan, to draw up a Five-Year Plan for the Central government. The princely states and provincial governments were expected to draw up their own plans.

Soon after Independence, the government set up the Advisory Planning Board in October 1947 with K.C. Neogy as chairman and assisted by some experts who had earlier served on the Bombay Plan, along with representatives from various ministers of the Central government and provincial governments.

It is thus striking that there was such a remarkable degree of agreement among various political and economic groups on the need for central economic planning and on its basic principles, despite the conflicting interests of political parties of different ideological persuasions, businessmen, labour leaders and experts from all over India.

There was also a large measure of agreement on the question of the activist-interventionist role of the government in economic planning and development. There was also a consensus on the question of active participation by the state in establishing basic and key industries, nationalization of financial institutions such as insurance companies and banks, and leaving the rest of the industries to the private sector, subjected to rigid supervision and control.

Most important of all, these plans and the debate that resulted created a national urge for planning. There was near unanimity on the necessity of central planning, in which the state would be an active party to accelerate social and economic development, and bring about a rapid rise in the standard of living. Economic planning was to be the first item of business on the national agenda after Independence.

No wonder then, it did not take even a year after Independence for the government to announce the national preference for planning with a dominant role for the state, and the institution of a Planning Commission. Thus, India became a pioneer among the developing countries of the Third World to initiate economic planning. In March 1950, the government of India set up the Planning Commission to formulate a plan, determine priorities, define the stages in which the plan should be carried out and propose the allocation of resources for due completion of each stage. The First Five-Year Plan was released in 1951. Interestingly, the basic functions assigned to the Planning Commission have remained more or less the same in the last five decades, by virtue of which it has formulated twelve Five-Year Plans, including the last one that began in 2012 but was aborted and replaced in 2014 by a new Three Year Action Agenda under the Modi-led government. Thus, since 2014, the Five-Year Plan, as we know it from 1951 to 2013, ended without anyone noticing it.

Five-Year Plans: The Key Component of Nehruvian Socialism

All the Five-Year Plans that have been formulated from 1951 have incorporated varying objectives and priorities. But the strategy underlying the attainment of the objectives has been remarkably the same: strengthening the public sector, which is the pillar of the Soviet economic strategy. Even the Ninth Plan (1997–2002) had the same strategy, although it was designed after the economic reforms had been in place for six years since 1991.

Earlier, the elaborate exercise for the preparation of a Five-Year Plan would begin with the consideration of the general approach to the Plan. Evaluation studies were undertaken with the help of the Programme Evaluation Organisation (PEO), Central Statistics Office (CSO) and various other institutions. The working groups and steering committees constituted by the Planning Commission for various sectors carried out exercises to provide inputs for the final formulation of the Plan.

The dimensions of the states' Plan were designed in consultation with individual state chief ministers. Simultaneously, discussions were also held with Central ministers to arrive at a public investment programme which was consistent with Plan priorities, known and anticipated constraints and resources available.

The Five-Year Plan document was also considered by the Union Cabinet and, thereafter, the final approval was given by the National Development Council (NDC), comprising members of the union council of ministers and state chief ministers and chaired by the prime minister.

The Plan would be implemented through the allocations made in Annual Plans. The formulation of the Annual Plan provided the Planning Commission with an opportunity to assess the previous year's Plan performance in various sectors and suggest 'course corrections' through a reorientation of policies and modifications of strategies.

That is, the general philosophy underlying all the Plans meant the active and direct participation of the government in the economy, combined with government control of economic institutions to empower itself to direct the market and command the economy. After the end of the Eighth Plan (1992–97), Five-Year Plans became a ritual of a statement of policies announced in the Budget session of the Parliament bereft of originality and relevance. The main new issues of economic reform were instead published as minister's or prime minister's statements. Thus, the Five-Year Plan died of natural causes in 2014 after the BJP came to power, and the Planning Commission was redefined and terminated, as we knew it earlier.

Hence, in this chapter, I have not considered the plans Ninth to Twelfth worthy of academic interest, in view of the economic reforms ushered in 1991, and progressive reduction of the state's primacy in economic decision-making.

Based on a study prepared by the Parliamentary Research Service (PRS) of the Lok Sabha, I give below a brief survey of these nine Plans. All of them have the following six characteristics of the Soviet economic strategy in different stages of dilution due to the exigencies of the situation:

i) Priority to capital goods sectors on the supposition that supply creates its own demand.

ii) Squeezing agriculture through taxes, terms of trade and credit-deposit ratios of government banks to raise funds for financing industry.

iii) Heavy taxes on consumption to curb it.

iv) Import substitution measures.

v) Controls and levies on finance such as of banks, insurances, etc.

vi) 'Commanding Heights' of the economy in the public sector, and a tight licencing system, where, except petty trade, every major economic activity needed government approval or participation. This included inputs for production, output for sale and availability of raw materials. Hence, it was referred to as Commanding Heights.

While that was the underlying philosophy, there are phases in the period when the fervour to favour the state's pre-eminence waxed and waned. The period 1951–65 saw the ascendancy of the state, with a national commitment to the concept of an active intervening state in the market. The period 1966–80 could be treated as one of national doubt, uncertainty and mixed signals, especially after the near-famine situation during 1965–68, and Prime Minister Lal Bahadur Shastri-initiated incentive-based agricultural growth that came to be known as the 'Green Revolution'. This was also the period of Mrs Indira Gandhi's tenure, during which radical steps such as nationalization of banks, coal industry and wholesale trade were undertaken. However, during 1980–90, which saw Mrs Gandhi's second term (1980–84) and Rajiv Gandhi's tenure as the prime minister (1985–90), there were major amendments made to the Soviet economic strategy, especially in encouraging foreign trade and taking loans from the international capital market, which, however, were mismanaged and led to the fiscal crisis of 1990–91. Between 1992 and 1996, the Government of Narasimha Rao as the prime minister deregulated the economy across the board but without making structural changes. Even today, economic policy is dominated by the thinking in the government that economic regulations can be liberalized, reduced and simplified but not necessarily abolished. That, unfortunately, is the unwavering mindset in India, where discipline means control, not incentives—for example, the decision of the government to set up the Ministry of Electronics and Information Technology

(MeitY) with venture capital funds at its disposal. There was no need for government involvement in this area, since information technology (IT) had grown hugely during 1990–2000 without any government assistance. Despite that, in the Ninth Plan (1997–2000), public investment was slated to grow at more than twice the growth rate of private investment, and nearly double the trend rate observed during 1980–90 (see Table 1).

Table 1

Growth Rates of Investment in Five-Year Plans

(per cent per annum)

	Trend Rate (1980–90)		Eighth Plan (1992–97)	Ninth Plan (1997–2002)
	Target	Actual	Corrected	Projected
Total Investment	6.4	10.3	5.9	7.3
Public Investment	6.3	2.5	2.5	11.5
Private Investment	6.5	14.4	7.2	5.5

Source: Ninth Plan (1997–2002), Vol. I (Table 2–23), Planning Commission, New Delhi, April

Since 1950, eight Five-Year Plans had been fully implemented. An Approach Document to the Ninth Five-Year Plan (1997–2002) was unanimously approved by the NDC in January 1997, but ended up being implemented as Annual Plans, and not a Five-Year Plan. The succeeding Five-Year Plans—Tenth, Eleventh and Twelfth—too were implemented as Annual Plans in the Union Budget.

In 2014, the Modi-led BJP government abolished the Planning Commission and created the NITI Aayog, which has generally functioned as a formality. Union and state budgets and the prime minister's ad hoc announcements have taken over the Five-Year

Plans, and generally and gradually market economics have become the central determinants of the economic trends.

A brief survey of the Five-Year Plans formulated and implemented till 2012 clearly reflects the pious formulation of objectives, and changing and shifting priorities, but most of all, no overall strategy or accountability for outcomes is exhibited.

Thus, briefly recapitulated, the First Five-Year Plan (1951–56) was called a 'ground preparing' exercise, which gave its primary attention to the achievement of economic stability and elimination of shortages of food and basic resources. Accordingly, it gave top priority to agriculture (including irrigation and power). About 44.6 per cent of the total outlay was allocated for agriculture.[15] The annual growth targeted in this Plan was 3.1 per cent of the national income. The Plan also aimed at increasing the rate of investment from 5 per cent to about 7 per cent of the national income.

The Second Five-Year Plan (1956–61) was structured on a Soviet economic model of growth authored by Feldman, and brought to India by P.C. Mahalanobis, while attributing it to this Soviet scholar, who was also disowned later by Stalin. Among other things, it aimed at a 25 per cent increase in the national income,[16] rapid industrialization with particular emphasis on development of basic and heavy industries, large expansion of employment opportunities, reduction of inequalities in income and wealth, and a more even distribution of economic power. The Plan laid stress on hastening industrialization with the aim of strengthening the capital base and productive capacity. It also aimed at increasing the rate of investment from about 7 per cent

---

[15]Sociology Discussion, 'Eradication of Poverty from India: Five-Year Plans, Rural Sociology', accessed on 28 June 2019, http://www.sociologydiscussion. com/poverty/eradication-of-poverty-from-india-five-year-plans-rural-sociology/2710
[16]Ibid.

of the national income to 11 per cent by 1960–61,[17] but it ignored the contribution of foreign trade.

The Third Plan (1961–66) aimed at securing a marked advance towards self-sustaining growth. Its objectives were to secure an increase in national income of over 5 per cent per annum and a simultaneous evolution of a pattern of investment capable of sustaining this rate of growth during subsequent Plan periods; achieve self-sufficiency in foodgrains (the target of foodgrain production stood at 100 million tons) and increased agricultural production to meet the requirement of industry and exports; expand basic industries such as steel, chemicals, fuel and power and establish machine-building capacity; fully utilize manpower resources and ensure a substantial expansion of employment opportunities; and establish greater equality of opportunity and bring about reduction in disparities of income and wealth and more equitable dispersal of economic power.

The implementation of the Fourth Plan was delayed on account of the India-Pakistan War in 1965, two successive years of severe drought, devaluation of the currency in 1966, general spurt in prices and the consequent erosion of resources available for the Plan. Therefore, three Annual Plans were formulated between 1966 and 1969, on an ad hoc basis.

The Fourth Five-Year Plan (1969–74) propounded the theme of accelerating the tempo of development with price stability, and reducing the fluctuations in agricultural production. The average annual rate of growth envisaged was 5.7 per cent. It laid special emphasis on reducing the concentration of economic power through wider diffusion of wealth and income.

The Fifth Plan (1974–79) aimed at achieving self-reliance and adoption of measures to raise consumption standards of the

---

[17]http://planningcommission.nic.in/plans/planrel/fiveyr/2nd/2planch1.html, accessed on 28 June 2019

people living below the poverty line. It also gave high priority to bringing inflation under control and achieving stability. The Plan targeted an annual growth rate of 5.5 per cent in national income and better capacity utilization of industries, developing renewable sources of energy, and integration of science and technology into the mainstream of development.

The Sixth Plan (1980–85) assigned the highest priority to the removal of poverty. The strategy was essentially to strengthen the infrastructure for both agriculture and industry so as to create conditions for a sustained and accelerated growth in output and exports. It aimed at meeting the minimum basic needs of the people through special programmes and by creating increased opportunities for employment, especially in the rural areas and the unorganized sector.

The Seventh Plan (1985–90) gave the highest priority to food, employment and productivity. Faster movement towards the objective of self-reliance with social justice was the core idea of this Plan. Its salient features were decentralized planning, maximum employment generation, self-sufficiency in food at higher levels of consumption, export-import balance, modernization and upgradation of technology. The Seventh Plan laid down an average growth rate target of 5 per cent. It also aimed at an 8.7 per cent annual growth rate for industries.

The Eighth Plan (1992–97) could not take off due to the fast-changing political situation at the Centre. By June 1991, the new government that assumed power at the Centre decided that the Eighth Plan would commence on 1 April 1992 and that 1990–91 and 1991–92 should be treated as separate Annual Plans. Formulated within the framework of the earlier approach to the Eighth Plan period (1990–95), the basic thrust of these two Annual Plans was on maximization of employment and social transformation.

The Approach Paper to the Ninth Plan, approved unanimously by the NDC in its meeting held on 16 January 1997, for the first time projected a GDP growth rate of 7 per cent per annum above the past Plans' target of 5–5.5 per cent of growth rate, including a growth rate of 4.5 per cent per annum in the agriculture sector. However, in February 1999, the new government led by Atal Bihari Vajpayee scaled down the targets (see tables 2 and 3). The 1997–99 Budgets proved to be major economic setbacks, because of the rapid change of the governments of prime ministers from P.V. Narasimha Rao (Congress) to Deve Gowda (United Front [1996–97]) and I.K. Gujral (United Front [1997–98]), within two years. Hence the approved estimates were reworked by the succeeding BJP government coalition (1998–99 to 2003–04) led by Prime Minister Vajpayee.

Table 2
Original Macro Parameters for the Ninth Plan (1997–2002)

(For a GDP growth rate of 7 per cent per annum)

	Eighth Plan	Ninth Plan	Post Plan
1. Domestic Savings Rate (% of GDP at market price)	24.1	26.2	27.2
2. Current Account Deficit (% of GDP at market price)	0.9	2.1	2.4
3. Investment Rate (% of GDP at market price)	25.0	28.3	29.5
4. ICOR	3.9	4.0	3.9
5. GDP Growth Rate (% Per Annum)	6.5	7.0	7.5
6. Export Growth Rate (% Per Annum)	10.3	14.5	14.5
7. Import Growth Rate (% Per Annum)	14.1	12.2	13.2

Source: Ninth Five-Year Plan (1977–2002), Vol. I, Planning Commission, April 1999
Note: ICOR is short for incremental capital output ratio. It is the inverse of the productivity of capital

Table 3

Revised Macro Parameters for the Ninth Plan (1997–2002)

	Eighth Plan	Ninth Plan	Post Plan
1. Domestic Savings Rate (% of GDP at market price)	23.8	26.1	27.2
2. Current Account Deficit (% of GDP at market price)	1.1	2.1	2.6
3. Investment Rate (% of GDP at market price)	24.9	28.2	29.8
4. ICOR	3.7	4.3	3.9
5. GDP Growth Rate (% Per Annum)	6.8	6.5	7.7
6. Export Growth Rate (% Per Annum)	11.9	11.8	14.5
7. Import Growth Rate (% Per Annum)	11.7	10.8	15.9

Source: Ninth Five-Year Plan (1997–2002), Vol. I, Planning Commission, April 1999

The objectives of the Ninth Plan originally arose from the Common Minimum Programme of the previous United Front government, the Chief Ministers' Conference on basic minimum services and the suggestions that had been put forward by the chief ministers of various states during extensive consultations.

The Eleventh Plan (2007–18 to 2012–13) of the UPA government had targeted an average annual growth of 9 per cent, higher than the realized rate of 7.6 per cent in the Tenth Plan (2002–07), but broadly in line with the acceleration of economic activity and growth experienced thereafter. The downturn in the global economy in 2011 due to the sovereign debt crisis in Europe combined with the emergence of domestic constraints on investment in infrastructure reduced the GDP growth to 6.2 per cent in 2011–12. As a result, the average growth over the five years of the Eleventh Plan was 7.9 per cent, and not 9 per cent as targeted. Achieving 7.9 per cent growth, the 2009–14 period represents a deceleration. In fact, from 2011–12, GDP growth showed a continuous deceleration till 2014, but after 2016,[18] it was also of decline.

Taken together, progressively over time and events, the national consensus and fervour for central planning had faded and now extinguished. The Plans have generally failed to meet their targets, and created more problems than have been solved during its implementation. This was to be expected, since the grafted Soviet model was alien to the Indian ethos, and was completely incompatible with the national economic endowment in terms of capital, labour, agriculture, industry and services.

A comparison of countries with a common history reveals that those countries that adopted the Soviet economic model performed much more poorly than their counterparts that had adopted the market economic strategy. Table 4 brings out this aspect by comparing East and West Germany, and North and South Korea.

Table 4
Economic Indicators South/North Korea (1995–96) and West/East Germany (1989) Compared

	Korea			Germany		
	South	North	South/ North ratio	West	East	West/ East ratio
Population million	44.9	23.9	1.9	62.1	16.6	3.8
GNP billion $	451.7	22.3	20.3	1,207	96	12.6
Per capita income $	10,067	957	10.5	19,283	5,840	3.3
Economic growth in % p.a. 1990–1995	+7.6	–4.5	–	3.0	-0.8	–
Government Expenditure billion $	97.1	19	5.1	547.7	61.8	8.9

[18]See Graph 1, page 134

contd...

	Korea			Germany		
	South	North	South/ North ratio	West	East	West/ East ratio
(as % of GNP)	(21.5)	85		(45.5)	(64.4)	
Defence expenditure						
billion $	14.4	5.2	2.8	28.5	11.2	2.6
(as % of GDP)	(3.2)	(23)		(2.4)	(11.6)	
per capita ($)						
Foreign trade						
billion $	260.2	2.05	126.9	611.1	47.0	13.0
(as % of GDP) per capita ($)	(57.6)	(9.2)		(50.6)	(49)	
Export of goods						
billion $	125.1	0.74	169	241.3	23.7	14.4
Import of goods						
billion $	135.1	1.31	103	269.8	23.3	11.5
Foreign debt						
billion $	79	11.8	6.6	106.7	22	4.9
(as % of GDP)	(17.5)	(53)		(8.8)	(23)	
Life expectancy						
in years (1995)	72.0	70.5	1.02	75.0	74.0	1.01
Infant mortality						
per 1,000 births (1995)	10	26	0.28	7.4	7.5	0.99
Rural population						
% of total (1995)	19	39	0.49	3.7	10.8	0.34
Radios[1]						
per 1,000 inhabitants (1989)	1,003	207	4.9	83%	99%	0.84
Televisions[2]						
per 1,000 inhabitants (1989)	207	14	14.8	94%	57%	1.65

Source: National Unification Board, Bank of Korea; StatistischesBundesamt, StatistischesJahrnuchder DDR; Weltbank

1: For West and East Germany: percentage of households with radio
2: For West and East Germany: percentage of households with colour television

What is a significant lesson to learn is that although free India from 1947 achieved a higher GDP growth following the Soviet economic strategy (1951–80) than under British imperialist rule (1870–1947), it nevertheless was at an unimpressive growth rate of 3.5 per cent per year in its period. It was only when liberalization and deregulation began in 1977, after the Janata Party government replaced more than three decades of Congress rule, that the growth rate rose from 3.5 per cent per year to 5 per cent (1977–80) and then from 5.5 per cent during the tenure of the Congress rule (1980–89) to nearly 7 per cent (1992–97) (see Table 5 below).

Table 5
Growth Performance in the Five-Year Plans

(Per cent per annum)

		Target	Actual
1 First Plan (1951–56)		2.1	3.61
2 Second Plan (1956–61)		4.5	4.27
3 Third Plan (1961–66)	Under	5.6	2.84
4 Fourth Plan (1969–74)	Soviet	5.7	3.30
5 Fifth Plan (1974–79)	Model	4.4	4.80
6 Sixth Plan (1980–85)	Planning	5.2	5.66
7 Seventh Plan (1985–90)		5.0	6.01
8 Eighth Plan (1992–97) Economic Reform		5.6	6.78

Source: Ninth Five-Year Plan (1977–2002), Vol. I, Planning Commission, April 1999

Note: The growth targets for the first three plans were set with respect to national income. In the Fourth Plan, it was Net Domestic Product. In all the Plans thereafter, GDP has been used. The Eighth Plan is based on the Quick Estimate for 1996–97

During the Phase 1 period, China, following a similar but more complete Soviet economic strategy, could not achieve a significantly higher growth rate than India, despite a huge investment effort and a wholesale transfer of complete plants and technology from the USSR. In this period, the Chinese growth rate was about 4 per cent per year, calculated after a reworking of Chinese official economic statistics which brought the data and concepts in conformity with the United Nations Statistical Office's standards. The ratio of Chinese output in physical comparable terms to Indian output is calculated and presented in Table 6. China, however, embarked upon economic reforms in 1980, ten years before India, and since then has been achieving a much higher growth rate, almost double compared to India.

Table 6
Ratio of Outputs: China to India, 1952–86

	Product	1952	1957	1967	1970	1978	1983	1986
1.	Rice	1.99	2.01	1.06	2.08	2.04	2.37	2.06
2.	Wheat	2.42	2.67	1.26	1.23	1.54	1.89	1.21
3.	Foodgrains	2.35	2.46	2.07	2.01	2.07	2.40	1.94
4.	Oilseeds	0.79	0.76	0.47	0.45	0.49	0.84	1.17
5.	Tea	0.27	0.32	0.26	0.81	0.45	0.69	0.45
6.	Milk	0.01	0.01	0.02	0.05	0.04	0.05	0.08
7.	Meat	5.23	6.65	8.22	9.74	9.84	12.75	14.01
I.	**Farm Output**	**2.03**	**2.27**	**2.13**	**2.28**	**2.30**	**2.82**	**2.26**
8.	Cotton Cloth	0.77	0.77	0.85	1.20	1.17	1.21	1.14
9.	Sugar	0.25	0.34	0.42	0.36	0.39	0.55	0.64
10.	Paper and Boards	2.72	1.22	3.09	3.09	4.35	6.24	6.01
11.	Light Bulbs	1.20	1.60	2.56	3.24	3.72	3.44	3.51
12.	Bicycles	0.67	1.03	1.13	1.81	2.43	4.42	5.83
13.	Radios	1.31	1.84	1.15	1.83	5.84	18.60	20.12
14.	TV Sets	0.00	2.00	4.00	1.20	0.86	4.34	3.72
15.	Sewing Machines	1.43	1.66	2.87	10.01	23.16	31.81	33.88
II.	**Light Industrial**	**0.80**	**0.92**	**1.72**	**2.17**	**3.54**	**5.63**	**6.12**

16.	Coal	1.68	3.00	3.30	4.64	6.09	5.13	5.23
17.	Crude Oil	1.01	3.47	2.43	4.51	8.97	4.10	4.14
18.	Electricity	1.20	1.70	2.04	2.08	2.50	2.63	2.40
19.	Natural Gas	0.15	0.29	1.50	1.99	4.88	2.05	2.09
III.	**Energy**	**1.61**	**3.03**	**3.16**	**4.37**	**6.83**	**4.79**	**4.76**
20.	Steel	1.25	2.55	1.87	2.69	3.19	3.93	3.84
21.	Cement	0.71	1.21	1.51	1.80	3.32	4.25	4.45
22.	Fertilizers	2.40	1.15	5.09	2.30	3.21	3.36	2.32
23.	Machine Tools	2.94	6.95	3.30	9.33	2.00	1.71	1.65
24.	Motor Vehicles	0.01	0.28	0.57	1.01	1.98	1.33	2.09
25.	Tractors	0.22	0.44	0.72	1.60	2.38	0.46	0.58
26.	Rail Wagons	0.84	1.22	0.09	1.24	1.46	0.99	1.42
IV.	**Heavy Industrial**	**1.75**	**2.02**	**2.04**	**3.02**	**3.63**	**2.72**	**2.78**
V.	**Total Output**	**1.51**	**1.66**	**1.94**	**2.51**	**3.26**	**3.87**	**3.77**
VI.	**Population**	**1.57**	**1.59**	**1.54**	**1.51**	**1.47**	**1.40**	**1.38**

Source: Data for China have been collected from diverse sources, including documents of Party Congress, The Ten Great Years, Beijing 1959, Statistical Year Book of China (1985), Beijing and U.S. Congress, Committee on Foreign Relations, Economic Development in India and China, 1956. Data for India: the 1986–87 (and earlier) Economic Survey, Ministry of Finance, New Delhi, February 1987

During the forty years of 'planned' economic development (1950–90), the economic strategy adopted by India had remained more or less unchanged. At the core, the strategy envisaged a large 'benign' government setting the pace of development through public-sector investments in Five-Year Plans, and by directing the volume of private-sector investments through the rigid state regulations on financial institutions, licencing, foreign exchange control and tax policy. Though India, in name, had been a mixed economy, in reality, it had been a state-directed economy—a hybrid 'command' economy, with the state having the commanding heights. There were significant changes made in this paradigm under Prime Minister Rao, but the quantum had been small and restricted to deregulation and not systemic change.

Even after the introduction of some deregulation measures by the Narasimha Rao government in the name of economic reform in 1991, the underlying 'command' economic structure was intact. India has still a considerable distance to go before it can be called a market economy. It is still to be dismantled, for which it requires a clear-cut commitment to 'second generation' reforms.

The results of this Soviet strategy have not been commensurate with either the resources mobilized from the public, or in terms of India's potential for growth. During the period from 1947 till 1991, the Indian economy had grown at the average rate of 4 per cent per year, while countries adopting a different strategy had achieved development in the same period, growing at 10–12 per cent per year. There is no reason for our low growth rate (well below 10 per cent per year), considering that we have the world's third-largest scientific and engineering manpower and had a high savings rate of 35± per cent of GDP. The so-called 'Four Tigers', namely South Korea, Taiwan, Hong Kong and Singapore, with less trained manpower and fewer natural resources, have moved from the Third World category to First World status (or Newly Industrialized Countries [NIC]) in just one generation! The per capita income of South Korea, for example, in 1962 was $82, comparable to India's $70 at that time. Today, South Korea's per capita income is about nine times that of India's current level. Even after allowing for certain advantages enjoyed by South Korea, such as assured markets in the US, there is no convincing explanation for the difference in performance of the two countries, except that the economic strategy was different.

It becomes important to understand the performance of the Soviet growth model of command economy during phases 1 and 2, and draw inferences as to why economic reforms became necessary in 1991. Between 1950 and 1980, i.e., over a thirty-year period, the average growth rate in GDP at factor cost at constant prices was a mere 3.5 per cent per year. Considering that the population growth rate during this period was 2.1 per cent per year, this meant that the per capita income grew at a dismal 1.4 per cent per year. At this rate, merely to double the per capita income, it would take fifty-one years of planning!

As Table 7 reveals, the agricultural sector during this thirty-year period had grown at the same level as the population growth rate of 2.1 per cent, which was highly unsatisfactory, while the service sector, including public utilities, grew at an impressive rate of 8 per cent. Electricity, gas and water services grew at an even faster rate of 9.5 per cent per year. The annual growth rate in the mining and manufacturing sector for the period was a modest 5 per cent.

Table 7

Sectoral Growth Rates of GDP at Factor Cost (1980–81 prices)

(per cent per annum)

Sector	1950–51 to 1989–90	1950–51 to 1980–81	1980–81 to 1989–90
1. Agriculture, Forestry and Fishing	2.3	2.1	2.9
2. Mining and Quarrying	4.9	4.5	6.5
3. Manufacturing	5.2	5.1	6.8
3.1 Registered	5.8	5.0	7.5
3.2 Unregistered	4.3	4.2	6.7
4. Electricity, Gas and Water	8.8	9.5	8.8
5. Other Services	7.2	6.8	7.6
Total GDP	3.7	3.5	5.2

Source: Economic Survey, Ministry of Finance, Figures from regression analysis

In retrospect, however, it is obvious from the result presented in tables 7 and 8 that less government control of the commanding heights of the economy produced more growth.

Table 8
Sectoral Shares in GDP at 1980–81 Prices (1950–51 to 1989–90)

(per cent)

Sector	1950–51	1965–66	1980–81	1985–86	1989–90
1. Agriculture, Forestry and Fishing	54.7	43.1	38.0	34.1	31.4
2. Mining and Quarrying	1.1	1.5	1.5	1.7	1.9
3. Manufacturing	11.4	16.7	17.7	20.0	21.0
3.1 Registered	5.4	9.5	10.0	12.3	13.1
3.2 Unregistered	6.0	7.2	7.7	7.6	7.0
4. Electricity, Gas and Water	0.3	0.9	1.6	2.0	2.2
5. Industry— (2) + (3) + (4)	12.8	19.1	20.8	23.7	25.1
6. Services	32.5	37.4	41.2	42.2	43.5
Total	100.0	100.0	100.0	100.0	100.0

Source: Uma Kapila (ed.), *Indian Economy Since Independence*, Academic Foundation, Delhi, 1999

Clearly, a 3.5 per cent growth rate in GDP, due to the Soviet model, however, was derisively called the Hindu rate of growth by the Left-wing economists (i.e. alleging Hindus are lazy and slow). This rate was significantly low and could not abolish poverty and unemployment within any time span, nor was it enough even to reduce it. In an early critical analysis of the Soviet command economic model (in *Indian Economic Planning:*

An Alternative Approach[19]), I had pointed to this bitter truth: that the 3.5 per cent growth rate would keep India poor, backward and, more importantly, make the nation fall further and further behind most of the fast-growing Asian countries. I had argued that India can and should target a 10 per cent growth rate, for which to be realized, the Soviet strategy ought to be jettisoned, deregulation and disinvestment should be carried out, and a market economy in which the government played a collaborative and not a hegemonic role should be adopted.

Perhaps this analysis was premature then, because the nation at that point in time was mesmerized by the view that more socialist control, not less, would improve the then current economic situation. This was the theme of Mrs Gandhi's campaign too, to sideline her 'secular Rightist' colleagues in the Congress party, such as Morarji Desai. Between 1969 and 1974, nationalization of industries and financial institutions was in vogue, and carried out systematically. In fact, Mrs Gandhi even gave up her father Jawaharlal Nehru's milder slogan of 'socialist pattern' of society with its preferred instrument of 'social control' for the more explicit slogan of 'socialism' and hard nationalization option. In that atmosphere, my thesis advocating a market economy was regarded as so off beam that even Mrs Gandhi, then the prime minister holding the portfolio of Finance, referred to my book on the floor of the Lok Sabha in her reply to the Budget debate in March 1970 to debunk it, of course, as the work of a 'Santa Claus with unrealistic ideas'.

If we contrast Phase 1 results with those of Phase 2 in Table 9, we get further support for the view that the less controlled and the more open the Indian economy was, the higher was the growth rate.

---

[19]Subramanian Swamy, *Indian Economic Planning: An Alternative Approach*, Vikas Publications, 1971

Table 9
Real GDP Growth Rates by Sector

(per cent per year)

	1950–60	1960–70	1970–80	1980–89
Agriculture	**2.7**	**1.5**	**1.7**	**2.6**
Agriculture	2.9	1.2	1.9	2.9
Forestry	0.3	3.3	–0.6	–3.9
Fishing	5.8	4.0	2.9	6.1
Industry	**6.0**	**5.5**	**4.7**	**7.4**
Mining & Quarrying	4.1	5.0	4.6	9.2
Manufacturing	6.1	4.7	4.9	8.0
Registered	7.2	5.6	4.8	9.7
Unregistered	5.1	3.7	5.0	5.6
Electricity, Gas & Water	10.2	11.5	7.4	9.8
Construction	5.9	6.9	3.1	3.1
Services	**4.1**	**4.4**	**4.6**	**6.2**
Transport, Storage, Communication	5.7	5.5	6.4	7.9
Trade, Hotels	5.1	4.5	4.9	5.3
Banking, Finance, Real Estate	3.2	3.1	4.4	6.2
Pub. Admn. & Defence	5.2	7.6	4.9	8.1
Other Services	2.9	4.0	2.8	5.0
GDP & Factor Cost	3.7	3.3	3.4	5.2

Source: Calculated by the author
Note: Least-squares growth rates. '1950–60' is 1950/51–1959/60, and similarly for other periods

During the Phase 2 years of 1980–90, the annual growth rate of GDP increased sharply to 5.2 per cent, as compared to 3.5 per cent earlier in Phase 1. Furthermore, in every sector, the growth rate was higher in Phase 2. If Phase 2 itself is further subdivided into 1980–85 and 1985–90, since in the latter period Prime Minister Rajiv Gandhi initiated a number of liberalization measures, the growth rate of GDP had accelerated. In the 1980–85 period, the growth rate had been 5 per cent, while in the later period (1985–90), it rose to 5.8 per cent. The same results were obtained for growth rates by sectors of economic activity as well. Clearly, taken together, i.e., the collapse of the Soviet Union and India's own experience and performance contrasted with China's, suggest that the Soviet economic strategy had not worked in India or anywhere else, including in the Soviet Union itself. The adoption of this model was thus the main cause for India's poor growth performance during 1950–80. Therefore, the Soviet economic strategy of reserving the commanding heights of the economy for the state with its systemic implications, had become an albatross around India's economic neck, and it was thus imperative that it be discarded for achieving full economic development. A command economy failed to deliver a high growth rate of 10 per cent, which was essential to solve India's main problems of poverty and unemployment.

This indictment of the Soviet economic strategy may be harsh, but a closer look at the strategy and model shows how untenable and unrealistic its fundamental assumptions have been for Indian conditions. It is truly amazing that Indian planners failed to understand this. Were they soft ideologues, or intellectually unwilling to understand the untenability, or for some obscure reason unwilling to see its absurdity for the Indian economic situation? There were certain fundamental assumptions of the Soviet economic strategy, as discussed below.

First, it was assumed that state intervention and control of the commanding heights of the economy would raise the level of domestic saving through higher public saving, and hence in investment as a whole. Furthermore, Feldman's two-sector model envisaged that the allocation of a large share of domestic saving as investment in the capital goods sector would raise the rate of growth and ultimately increase consumption more rapidly than otherwise, after a period. For example, a one-third share of domestic saving allocated to the capital goods sector would, after fifteen years, raise the consumption levels above and beyond that obtained with lower shares for allocation of investment.

The fundamental error in this assumption was that while investment in the capital goods sector would increase production in that sector, the resultant output was expected to be purchased by other sectors, especially the consumer goods sector. However, due to a lack of purchasing power, this did not happen. The consumer goods sector in real life did not find it profitable to buy these capital goods, and thus all that was achieved was excess idle capacity in that sector.

Even the expectation that public savings would surge proved to be false because the public-sector enterprises by the very nature of their structuring were inefficient and loss-making. Public-sector savings did not increase at all, and on the contrary, declined as a ratio to GDP from 1965–66. It was the household saving that surged to double as a ratio to GDP. By nationalization and capturing of the commanding heights, public investment instead increased by drawing on the household saving through financial institutions, banks and provident fund. The government, thereby, cornered 81 per cent of the investible funds.

Second, it was assumed that because of a large investment in the public sector, the growth rate would accelerate. This did not happen. The growth rate stagnated between 1950 and 1980, around 3.5 per cent per year because of non-market, inefficient decision-making by the government on the allocation of investment and management of funds. Hence, the incremental capital-output ratio (ICOR) rose year after year (see Table 10) with increasing investment, peaking in 1980, the last year of the adherence to the closed Soviet model.

Table 10
ICORs by Sector

	1950–60	1960–70	1970–80	1980–89
Agriculture	**2.0**	**4.7**	**5.4**	**3.5**
Agriculture	2.0	6.0	2.1	3.1
Forestry	2.2	0.4	ND	ND
Fishing	2.9	3.5	4.6	2.6
Industry	**4.2**	**6.0**	**7.7**	**5.5**
Mining & Quarrying	2.8	4.8	10.3	8.5
Manufacturing	4.3	7.0	6.9	4.0
Registered	(6.9)	(9.0)	(9.0)	(4.1)
Unregistered	(1.0)	(3.1)	(4.0)	(3.8)
Electricity, Gas & Water	16.3	15.2	18.5	15.7
Construction	1.2	1.5	3.1	4.0
Services	**6.1**	**5.7**	**5.3**	**4.2**
Transport, Storage, Communication	12.8	14.6	8.8	6.5
Trade, Hotels	1.6	1.4	3.2	3.7
Banking, Finance, Real Estate	10.0	9.8	6.2	5.0
Pub. Admn. & Defence	10.9	6.0	7.4	4.3
Other Services	2.4	2.2	2.4	1.7
GDP & Factor Cost	3.9	5.7	6.2	4.7

Source: Based on data provided by the Ministry of Finance to International Finance Agencies. 1950–60 is 1950/51–1959/60, and similarly for other periods.
Note: Capital output ratios shown in this table are obtained by dividing average real investments as a share of real gross value added at factor cost in each period by the corresponding rate of growth of real gross value added at factor cost. These estimates are not directly comparable to estimates which value output at market prices instead of factor cost. ND is 'not defined' due to negative output growth over the corresponding period.

Different sectors have different ICORs. For example, sectors such as steel, aluminium, copper, petrochemicals and refineries are highly capital- and energy-intensive, while the power sector itself is the most capital-intensive. Other sectors, such as agriculture, fishery, forestry, animal husbandry, construction, and services such as trade, education and health services, require much less capital per unit of output produced by them (see Table 10). The labour-intensive sectors have a low ICOR, which means that the capital requirement is low and the employment potential is high.

The ICOR of individual sectors can be reduced by increasing efficiency in the use of resources within these sectors. However, even if sectoral productivity cannot be altered, the overall ICOR can be reduced by changing the investment mix, i.e., investing more in low ICOR sectors. In this way, with the same rate of investment as at present, viz., 24 per cent of the GDP, the Indian economy can reduce the ICOR to 3 and achieve a GDP growth rate of 8 per cent per annum (and an employment growth rate of about 5 per cent per annum). If the rate of investment can be raised to 30 per cent, then a 10 per cent growth rate can be achieved. This means that we can achieve near-full employment and eliminate poverty in the next ten to twelve years, depending on whether an 8 per cent or a 10 per cent growth rate is targeted.

This would naturally require a restructuring of the investment pattern, for example, more investment in education, health and family welfare, massive construction activity, electrification for all villages, and rapid development of agriculture, fisheries, forestry and light industries, which will generate higher growth and more employment opportunities and more exports. This would also improve the quality of life. A lower growth rate of population as a consequence of better education/awareness and health to, say, 1.5 per cent per annum, and a higher GDP growth rate of up to 10 per cent per annum will mean a rate of growth of per capita income of 8.5 per cent per annum against the average of 1.5 per cent for forty years (1950–90). With this rate of growth, we can nearly double the per capita income in eight and a half years.

Third, it was erroneously supposed that a strict regime of import control and import substitution would reduce our foreign dependence and enable the economy to become self-sufficient. This was regardless of whether India had the 'comparative advantage' in producing that particular item. To facilitate import substitution, protection through very high tariff walls and outright bans had been provided to the Indian producer without a time limit, so much so as to not allow any import if the items were or could be produced within the country, even if only in a monopoly! Since there was a ban on importing a similar item once produced in the country, even if the market was small, there was practically a guarantee of making profits, for the price was fixed on a cost-plus basis, and the unequal distribution of income ensured enough buyers to make the production beat the break-even point.

In such a policy environment, there was hardly any selectivity. While the gain from such a policy was that India produced a whole range of industrial products—from pins to planes, practically all consumer items, basic inputs, capital goods, and highly capital- and energy-intensive items—what we lost was the price and quality that could have come from competition, and therefore the tax-paying consumer became the ultimate loser.

It was thus a fundamental error of assumption in the closed Soviet economic model that a strict import substitution policy, without regard to comparative advantage in costs, would pave the way for industrialization and self-reliance. Therefore, in 1991, the time had come to take a fresh look at this policy, by virtue of which the Indian economy had become a high-cost economy, and which made it difficult for Indian producers to compete in external markets. The policy of import substitution had run its disastrous course; there was not much logic for blind import substitution in the first place, and there was even less in 1991 after the Uruguay Round had laid the foundation for free trade and the World Trade Organization (WTO).

The fourth argument that had been trotted out for adopting the Soviet economic strategy and reserving the commanding heights of the economy for state control was that such a system would produce an egalitarian economic order and equitable distribution of income and wealth. This never happened in the first fifteen years of planning, nor did we see that happen thereafter. On the contrary, the inequalities increased, and wealth distribution was skewed. The regulations, the licencing system, quota schedules, legislations, nationalization of industries and financial institutions, land reform and quantitative restrictions on international trade, all together became a device for blocking competition, cost-cutting and avoiding economies of scale. Adventurers and pirate entrepreneurs with access to politicians (because of election-funding), were able to get captive markets, government concessions and uneconomic subsidies. They made a quick profit using the maze of regulations which controlled the entry of competitors. Furthermore, the complexity of licencing and land legislations led to corruption, which further undermined the thrust to achieve whatever the stated goals and aims of planning had been. In other words, socialist controls created near-monopolistic situations instead of the intended dispersal of economic power and lessening of inequality.

Most importantly, it was a monumentally false assumption that rapid growth of the capital goods industry by cutting consumption and diverting savings would modernize agriculture. Thereafter, it was assumed that agriculture could be squeezed of funds in the medium term through adverse terms of trade and by the reversal of the credit-deposit ratio in banks, to finance this type of Soviet-style industrialization. But, as mentioned earlier, agriculture had already been squeezed of funds and starved of investments for almost two centuries by a British imperialist policy of land revenue. Hence, the sector was in urgent need of investments so that it could generate income and purchasing power, and be in a position to serve as a market for commodities produced in the industrial sector. Between 1950 and 1970, the growth rate of foodgrains, for example, slumped, necessitating huge imports (see tables 11, 12 and 13), especially during 1965–69. The ensuing crisis crafted the Green Revolution for India, which was initiated by Prime Minister Lal Bahadur Shastri in 1965, and taken forward by Agriculture Minister C. Subramaniam, assisted by the director of the Indian Council of Agricultural Research (ICAR), M.S. Swaminathan, who devised the package of optimum amounts of fertilizers, pesticides, quality seeds and bank loans. By 1975, India, thus, became self-sufficient in foodgrains. Hence, the term 'Green Revolution', although it touched only the top 10 per cent of the farmers. The remaining 90 per cent still await being catered to.

Table 11
Annual Compound Growth Rates of Foodgrains Production
(Base Triennium ending 1981–82=100)

(Per cent per annum)

Crop	1950–51 to 1959–60	1960–61 to 1969–70	1970–71 to 1979–80	1980–81 to 1989–90
Rice	3.28	–8.05	1.91	4.29
Wheat	4.51	5.90	4.69	4.24
Coarse Cereals	2.75	1.48	0.74	0.74
Total Cereals	3.0	2.51	2.37	3.63
Pulses	2.72	1.35	–0.54	2.78
Total Foodgrains	3.22	1.72	2.08	3.54

Source: Economic Survey, Ministry of Finance, 1995–99, New Delhi

Table 12
Quinquennium Rates for Growth of Foodgrains Production
(1965–70 to 1985–90)

Quinquennium	Quinquennium Average Production of Foodgrains (in million tonnes)	Average Annual Compound Growth–Rate, Compared with the Average of the Previous Quinguennium
1965–70	87.01	–
1970–75	103.02	3.44
1975–80	120.04	3.11
1980–85	138.06	2.84
1985–90	155.19	2.37

Source: Economic Survey, 1989

But even this 'revolution' without the backing of sustained investment began to peter out, as Table 12 shows, despite unmistakable productivity gains (see Table 13).

Table 13
Growth Performance of Food Crops and
Non-food Crops (1952–92)

(Per cent per annum)

	1952–53 to 1964–65	1968–69 to 1981–82	1981–82 to 1991–92
Food Crops	Pre-Green Revolution	Post-Green Revolution	
Area	0.98	0.37	−0.26
Yield	1.51	1.85	3.19
Output	2.51	2.21	2.92
Non-food crops			
Area	2.30	1.06	1.71
Yield	1.66	1.34	2.55
Output	3.99	2.41	4.30

All Crops			
Area	1.21	0.54	0.49
Yield	1.77	1.74	2.93
Output	3.01	2.29	3.43

Source: 'India at 50', *The Indian Express,* 1997, New Delhi

Because of this, as Table 14 will show, agriculture could not absorb the fast-growing labour force (at 4 per cent per year). This forced a sizeable migration of landless and unskilled labour in search of employment to cities, clogging urban centres with slums and shantytowns. According to the World Bank (1998) studies, the total factor productivity growth may have become negative in the 1990s, which shows that a mere rise in capital investment and labour force employment by economic deregulation is sufficient to sustain a high growth rate for long. Long-term acceleration in GDP growth rate requires innovations in the techniques of production.

Table 14
Growth Rates for Employment by Major Sectors

Sector	1973–74 to 1977–78	1977–78 to 1983	1983 to 1987–88
Agriculture	2.32	1.20	0.65
Mining	4.68	5.85	6.16
Manufacturing	5.10	3.75	2.10
Construction	1.59	7.45	13.69
Electricity, gas and water supply	12.23	5.07	4.64
Transport, storage and communication	4.85	6.35	2.67
Other services	3.67	4.69	2.50
Total	2.82	2.22	1.55

Source: Arun Ghosh, 'Eighth Plan: Challenges and Opportunities,' *Economic & Political Weekly,* Vol. 26, Issue No. 17, 27 April 1991

The serious aspect of the unemployment situation was the progressive reduction in the growth of employment in the organized public and private sector. According to figures available (see Table 15), not only did the employment growth rate in the organized sector decline, but in the organized private sector, the employment growth for some years was negative in the 1980s. Considering that the demand for jobs in the organized sector was growing at about 4 per cent per year, a 2.2 per cent per year increase in jobs is woefully inadequate.

Table 15
Growth of Employment

	Organized sector (in lakhs)	Unorganized sector (in lakhs)	Total
1983	240.1	2785.9	3026.0
1990–91	270.6	3297.0	3567.6
1997–98	282.5	3546.0	3828.5
Growth rate of employment*			
1983 to 1990–91	1.73	2.41	2.39
1990-91 to 1997–98	0.60	1.10	1.70

Source: *Approach to the Ninth Five-Year Plan*, Planning Commission, February 1998, New Delhi

*Annual average in per cent

This problem has been further complicated by the structure of investments made during the Sixth and Seventh Plans. Agriculture, which employed about 70 per cent of the labour force, had received declining real public investment during the 1980s, at the alarming rate of minus 2 per cent per year. In other words, agriculture was in no position to absorb more labour due to the lack of adequate investment, while the organized sector in urban areas, which received a lion's share of the public investment, failed to generate sufficient employment to absorb the surplus labour. If it were not for the unorganized sector, which did its bit, the situation on the unemployment front would have been explosive.

This double squeeze on employment continues even today, which represents a major failure of policy. We, therefore, have to restructure our economic strategy to ensure that employment generation becomes a high priority of policymaking. Correct policy initiatives would help achieve full employment in the next ten years. In particular, keeping due regard for environmental needs, pollution control and decongestion of cities, it is imperative that we restructure investment. This should be done to accord priority to agricultural modernization, so that we not only have a higher output, but also generate enough employment to usefully absorb the labour force on non-crop activities, thus relieving the pressure on cities.

If proper restructuring of the economic strategy is effected, and it leads to a higher growth rate and employment, then it becomes imperative to fashion a dynamic export policy which not only makes it possible to sell our surpluses abroad, but also to finance required additional imports and liquidate our acquired foreign debt. Besides, if the targeted commodities for exports are carefully chosen, then exports can be the vehicle for agricultural modernization, industrialization and economic development in general.

Under the influence of the Soviet model-makers, we had regarded exports as a kind of necessary evil to be indulged in order to be able to earn foreign exchange to purchase goods by import. The Gandhian goal of self-reliance had been misunderstood to be tantamount to self-sufficiency. In other words, we sought to produce everything that we could, and the items that we could not, we strived to produce sometime in the future through an enforced programme of import substitution.

Of the five fundamental assumptions that went wrong with the Soviet economic model in India, I regard the miscalculation in agriculture as the most crucial and damaging to long-term growth prospects. This miscalculation also represents a huge opportunity missed, because Indian agriculture is endowed with land, water, soil fertility and a distinct comparative advantage in costs that can make the country a low-cost granary of the world. Not only that, using the advanced mathematical technique of Spectral Analysis Using Fourier Transforms (used by me in another publication) on a century of index number of prices data, reveals that when all is said and done, agricultural prices lead the general price level with a lag of two years. Stabilizing agricultural prices, in other words, meant controlling general inflation in the economy, a lesson of crucial importance.

Thus, an inflation control policy which concentrates on stabilizing agricultural prices alone can simultaneously control general and non-agricultural prices. A policy that fails to influence the agricultural prices thus will fail to control any prices in India, irrespective of how much development planning textbook support there may be to argue otherwise. Ironically, the last fifty years of planning and inflation experience have failed to persuade the bureaucrats of the government of India of their conceptual error, and I don't suspect spectral analysis will fare any better with them. Suppressing, denying, squeezing and taxing agriculture have been the cultural constants in the Finance Ministry, all to the nation's cost. This despite the fact that for two decades (1960–80), real wages in agriculture remained stagnant in constant prices, while in manufacturing and the public sector, it had doubled, as Table 16 shows.

Table 16
Real Wages in the Selected Sectors of Indian Economy

Year	Agriculture	Organized Manufacturing (a)		Public Sector (b)
		Prod. Wage	Real Wage	
	(1)	(2)	(3)	(4)
1960/61	1.43	6.40	6.40	
1961/62	1.51	6.80	6.64	
1962/63	1.48	7.12	6.80	
1963/64	1.28	7.44	6.80	
1964/65	1.37	7.84	6.40	
1965/66	1.32	7.84	6.56	7.4
1966/67	1.25	8.40	6.88	7.7
1967/68	1.24	8.80	6.64	7.7
1968/69	1.47	9.04	6.88	8.0
1969/70	1.49	9.76	7.84	9.0
1970/71	1.58	10.16	8.32	9.9
1971/72	1.59	9.84	8.32	10.4
1972/73	1.48	n.a.	n.a.	8.4
1973/74	1.32	10.56	8.80	7.9
1974/75	1.18	10.00	8.08	8.1
1975/76	1.49	10.96	9.12	9.3
1976/77	1.68	11.12	10.00	10.1
1977/78	1.62	11.52	9.68	10.4
1978/79	1.68	12.08	10.32	11.4
1979/80	1.52	11.92	10.80	11.9
1980/81				12.2
1981/82				12.2
1982/83				12.7
1983/84				13.5
1984/85				14.1

Source: R. Lucas, *India's Industrial Policy*, Boston University, 1986, Center for Monitoring Indian Economy, Basic Statistics Relating to Indian Economy, various issues

Note: Real wages are derived by deflating the corresponding nominal figures by the Consumer Price Index of Industrial workers, except for Column 2. Figures in Column 2 are derived by deflating nominal wages by wholesale price index for manufactured products.

(a) Refers to ASI Census sector averaged for both public and private sectors.

(b) Wages averaged for industrial and commercial undertaking, including banks.

Spearheading the Reform Movement

By the late 1980s, the consensus in the nation had shifted. The news about poverty in the USSR (which had filtered out due to Glasnost), the switching to market reforms in China and the new status of Indian residents in the US as a community with the highest per capita income amongst all American communities, influenced the people in India to ask whether the Soviet economic strategy was, after all, a misfit in the Indian economic situation. Recognizing this, I moved a resolution in the Parliament in August 1988, which is as follows:

RAJYA SABHA

LIST OF BUSINESS

Friday, 5 August 1988

11 A.M.

PRIVATE MEMBERS' BUSINESS (RESOLUTIONS)

Shri Subramanian Swamy to move the following Resolution: Considering the unimpressive economic performance during the last forty years in our country and taking into account the experience of China and the USSR, this House urges upon the Government to abandon the Soviet economic strategy adopted earlier and instead formulate the Eighth Five-Year Plan on the economic model shaped by the postulates of Mahatma Gandhi, Sardar Patel, Jayaprakash Narayan and Chaudhary Charan Singh, in general, and the principles of economic decentralization and self-reliance, in particular, with the main thrust on the need to motivate people for self-employment by providing them adequate incentives and opportunities with a view to:

I.   Generate a growth rate of ten per cent per year by placing more emphasis on agriculture, employment generation and ensuring optimum utilization of available resources through the effective use of market forces and fiscal policy; and

II. Making India a fully developed country within one generation.

It is one of the great ironies of this grafted Soviet economic strategy that in the name of upholding the principles of self-reliance and fighting monopolies, what really had been achieved in forty years in Indian planning was the opposite; besides a debt-trap and inefficient captive markets to boot. In 1991, after witnessing the failure of the Soviet model of economic growth within the country, and abroad in what used to be the Soviet Union itself (not to mention East Europe), it was obviously time to consider an alternative model.

This alternative model or new economic strategy naturally could not be a copy of what is prevalent in the US or Western Europe (known popularly as the capitalist model). The reason for this was simple. The latter countries have a relative surplus of capital and therefore high labour costs. Hence the approach in these countries is to save on the utilization of labour through the use of highly automated capital intensive technology. In India, we can effectively use labour in greater measure to reduce costs and enhance production, and thus in many areas do without such highly automated labour-saving technology. This was the essence of Mahatma Gandhi's philosophy, which was dubbed as 'anti-modern.' The factor endowment in India, that is the ratio and availability of capital labour knowledge mix, is different from the developed countries and other developing countries. This fact called for a uniquely different response to the development paradigm in India. It had to be India-specific.

In Phase 3, in a significant but not complete departure from the command economy concept, economic reforms were implemented by the Narasimha Rao government in 1991, in which I held Cabinet position till 1996. The blueprints for these reforms and its parameters were, however, prepared during my tenure in the previous government as commerce minister (in the period 1990–91). The mere fact that Prime Minister Rao was able to set in place these reforms within ten days of his taking office attests to the fact that the position papers on reforms were prepared much earlier and ready for implementation. That he did implement, goes to his credit. In fact, some disinvestment of public-sector undertaking (PSU) share was included, at my insistence in the Cabinet meeting held in January 1991, in the aborted 1991–92 general budget, proposals of which were presented to Parliament in February 1991. Obviously impressed, Prime Minister Rao appointed me as Chairman, with Cabinet Minister Rank, of a Commission to study the WTO/new General Agreement on Tariffs and Trade (GATT) proposals and also the debate on Labour Standards, even though I was not a member of his party, nor was Janata Party a coalition ally of the Congress party.

4

ROAR OF THE 'CAGED' TIGER

Nowhere else, not even in Communist China or the Soviet Union, is the gap between what might have been achieved and what has been achieved as great as in India.

—'A Survey of India', *The Economist* (4 May 1991)[20]

Soviet-style socialism (1950–91) is the undisputed cause in India for this monumental loss of opportunity since 1947. Its after-effects are felt even today, since it warped the mentality of Indians towards making profit and the necessity of fair competition. No greater misfortune had befallen India than the unthinking acceptance or even capitulation of Indian intellectuals and elite for over five decades, to the (now-collapsed and discredited) Soviet-inspired model of command economy. The economic policy in this model was embedded in an unbelievably

---

[20]'A Survey of India', *The Economist*, 4 May 1991, p. 5, accessed on 27 April 2019, https://www.dispatchesfromindia.com/uploads/1/0/5/0/105088669/dispatches-from-india_india-before-1991.pdf

complicated system of controls and restraints that became the despair of the enterprising, and the happy hunting ground for the unscrupulous.

However, an important reason for the failure of the concept that had been favoured by Nehru and the Leftists can be traced to India's national ethos, which is based on individualism and has its roots in a composite Hindu culture. The social consciousness that prevails in such an ethos is one that seeks harmony with nature. An economic philosophy consistent with this ethos was admirably formulated by Mahatma Gandhi during the freedom struggle, but of the then top leaders, only Sardar Patel and C. Rajagopalachari enthusiastically owned it and was subsequently incorporated by Deendayal Upadhyaya in his Integral Humanism. Although Nehru did not have the courage during Gandhi's lifetime to openly challenge it, he never did subscribe to it.

If an individualistic, democratic society is to be strong, then the economy must help secure jobs to foster the spirit of self-reliance and rational risk-taking. The correct economic policy is one that is largely based on the use of the market mechanism, with the government as an umpire in the clash of demand and supply forces and as an enlightened patron, guiding market forces to equilibrium by incentive whenever distortions take place. Such an incentive-based market system is also in consonance with the Indian cultural values of individualism and collective harmony.

I do not advocate laissez faire (free enterprise) because in it there is a very small role for the government, but I do favour market economy based on fair competition with transparent rules and laws. The government (in such a market-driven policy) would have a role, no doubt, but it would be primarily to correct market malfunction, promote minimum standards of living and generally act as an umpire in the interaction between consumers and producers in the marketplace and a police person against the corrupt. The government would also have to calibrate money supply to contain inflation and interest rates, levy fair taxation and influence by inducements the investments that promote growth, innovation and employment. It would have the right to intervene in the market to give protection to those who cannot survive unfair competition, to create a level playing field for industries, promote exports, provide enabling infrastructure, give enlightened and infrastructural support to small producers, and arrange marketing facilities for farmers and rural enterprise. In such an economy, the government will certainly have no right to occupy the 'commanding heights' of the economy.

By 1991, India had achieved a modest average growth rate of less than 4 per cent per annum over four decades, despite the diligent Indian people raising the rate of saving from a low 5 per cent of GDP in 1951 to one of the world's highest saving rates of 22 per cent of GDP in the late 1980s. Had we utilized this investment resource efficiently, as Japan and the East Asian tigers did during the 1975–95 period (of maintaining a capital output ratio of 2.2), the growth rate of the economy would have indeed been 10 per cent per year, and with it full employment and large reduction in poverty would have been achieved over two decades. India's performance, instead, was poor, compared with Japan, South Korea and Taiwan, among others. These countries had achieved 10 per cent or higher growth rate even over a stretch of twenty years, leaving India far behind.

Another reason for dissatisfaction with the less than 4 per cent growth rate is that none of our pressing problems, such as poverty and unemployment, can be solved if the economy progresses at this rate or any rate below 10 per cent. By all objective accounts, during the last seven decades, the percentage of people living below the poverty line had not gone down, despite twelve large Five-Year Plans. Unemployment, in fact, had increased, and perhaps is still increasing in number.

The investment strategy was obviously grossly inefficient, considering that a quadrupling of the rate of saving did not raise the growth rate. It is imperative to understand this squandering of resources, the mismanagement and misdirection in detail, before we can assess the economic reforms carried out since 1991, and formulate what needs to be done further from now on.

Thus, growth rate of the economy could have been much higher, had we used our resources efficiently. In fact, what took place was a staggering squandering of resources. While in the early 1950s, about ₹2 of investment could generate an annual income of ₹1; in 1991, more than ₹6 was required to generate the same income.

This squandering had been done in the name of socialism. The government's increasing control on resources had merely meant decreasing accountability of the same—money down the drain, so to speak. Public-sector investment was 60 per cent of the total, but its contribution to saving was only 7.5 per cent. The government had cornered 81 per cent of the investible resources. This was because of the Soviet strategy of squeezing resources out of agriculture and other sectors to finance 'heavy' or capital-intensive industries.

Socialism has now failed worldwide because a large government not only meant poor accountability, but also a numbing of incentives. The governments in China, at one stage the most fanatical believers in the concept of omnipotent government, under the leadership of Deng Xiaoping, accepted this bitter truth and reoriented their policies to give incentives a pride of place in their economic strategy, despite their disdain for multiparty democracy. I was privileged to be invited to visit China and meet Chairman Deng Xiaoping, and did so on 8 April 1981 in a hundred-minute one-on-one meeting.

Socialism means a large government, and a large government needs finances through heavy taxation. And nothing kills incentive as unthinking taxation does. On the other hand, those governments which founded their economic strategy on the cornerstone of incentives based on reasonable taxation of the individual have produced miracles. Beginning with Japan, South Korea, Taiwan and even tiny islands such as Hong Kong and Singapore, which have little natural resources, have put countries such as India and China to shame by their growth performance. A war-devastated Japan was able to become a developed country in twenty-five years; Hong Kong, Taiwan and South Korea became industrialized nations in eighteen years; while Thailand, Indonesia and the Philippines are also on the way to that status. Each of these small Asian countries had achieved growth rates exceeding 10 per cent, and full employment as well. Thus, it is only legitimate to enquire why India had not managed to become a developed country even in the forty years since 1950.

The proponents of heavy progressive taxation have argued in the past on the need to redistribute incomes for greater equity. Though in theory, this is an acceptable argument, in practice, no government in the world has been able to set up a tax-collecting machinery to achieve this redistribution effectively. On the contrary, the international experience is that progressive taxation, which goes against the healthy acquisitive spirit of the individuals, ends up being corrupted, and thus corrupting everything else.

We must recognize that in a country like India, it is not possible to achieve equity through progressive taxation. We have tried it, and it has failed. The only practical way to achieve equity in India is to create adequate employment and ensure certain minimum amenities for those employed, in terms of housing, education and transportation. The taxation system should be used as an instrument to give incentives to capitalists for providing all these facilities.

With their long commercial history and culture, Indians cannot be inspired or deterred by suffocating regulations. If the government-imposed controls and regulations go against the individual's incentive and good sense, the average Indian will subvert it and render ineffective these restrictions. That is what was witnessed earlier. The pity is that in such a climate, the honest are suppressed and the system then provides a premium to the brigands and the pirates. Moral degeneration inevitably follows.

The command economy, in which the government has an interventionist and domineering role, had clearly failed us by 1990. Hence, for the economy to really prosper, a clean break from the old strategy was essential.

The basic shift that India needed to make was, therefore, in the structure of decision-making for the efficient allocation of resources—to shift from the centralized hybrid command economy to a decentralized market economy in which decisions are made by economic units freely, provided certain parameters of a national social welfare policy are adopted by the Parliament and enforced through the executive.

The Triggers

The superficially impressive growth performance in the late 1980s ironically ushered in economic reforms. The country ran into a serious macroeconomic crisis by the end of that era that culminated in accelerating inflation and creating a critical balance of payments crisis in early 1991. Although there has been a fair amount of publicity given to the fact that the growth rate during the 1980s, during Rajiv Gandhi's tenure as the prime minister, was well above the rate achieved (see Table 1), nevertheless, the cost of achieving this higher growth rate has been excessively large.

Table 1
Real GDP Growth Rates by Sector

(per cent per year)

	1950–60	1960–70	1970–80	1980–89
Agriculture	**2.7**	**1.5**	**1.7**	**2.6**
Agriculture	2.9	1.2	1.9	2.9
Forestry	0.3	3.3	–0.6	–3.9
Fishing	5.8	4.0	2.9	6.1
Industry	**6.0**	**5.5**	**4.7**	**7.4**
Mining & Quarrying	4.1	5.0	4.6	9.2
Manufacturing	6.1	4.7	4.9	8.0
Registered	7.2	5.6	4.8	9.7
Unregistered	5.1	3.7	5.0	5.6
Electricity, Gas & Water	10.2	11.5	7.4	9.8
Construction	5.9	6.9	3.1	3.1
Services	4.1	4.4	4.6	6.2
Transport, Storage, Communication	5.7	5.5	6.4	7.9
Trade, Hotels	5.1	4.5	4.9	5.3
Banking, Finance, Real Estate	3.2	3.1	4.4	6.2
Pub. Admn. & Defence	5.2	7.6	4.9	8.1
Other Services	2.9	4.0	2.8	5.0
GDP & Factor Cost	3.7	3.3	3.4	5.2

Source: Calculated by the author
Note: Least-squares growth rates. '1950–60' is 1950/51–1959/60, and similarly for other periods.

The costs have been in terms of destabilized macroeconomic balances, especially the fiscal and balance of payment deficits, pushing the economy perilously close to the double debt traps (internal and external), doubling the foreign indebtedness ($71 billion) making us the third most indebted nation in the world and drying up exchange reserves (to less than one month of imports). All this had pushed India to become a high-cost economy and internationally uncompetitive. The NRI deposit (nearly ₹20,000 crore) was the thin thread that kept us from falling into the ignoble pit of loan repayment default and from the complete collapse of our international credit rating. Indeed, this state of affairs had been brought about by unthinking 'liberalization' of the economy, which meant unrestricted imports, reckless short-term borrowing from abroad and little concern for exports.

The growth during the late 1980s was achieved by a sustained record of investment, which rose to about 22.7 per cent of the GDP on an average during this period. However, the savings rate, although constantly rising, averaged 20.3 per cent during the same period, thus leaving a substantial investment-savings gap of about 2.4 per cent of the GDP over this five-year period. Much of this savings-investment gap was accounted for by the negative governmental savings of about 1.6 per cent of the GDP. This domestic economic imbalance during the late 1980s reflected itself in a current account deficit (CAD) of 3.3 per cent of the GDP, which became increasingly unsustainable. Short-term foreign debt rose from $2.2 billion in 1985 to $5.7 billion in 1991, becoming 7 per cent of total foreign debt, half of which was concessional loans from international financial institutions. India, which owed only $2.3 billion to private creditors in 1980, now owed $22.8 billion in 1989–90. Debt-servicing sharply increased to 31 per cent (1989–90), compared to 13.6 per cent in 1984–85. Interest payments on external debt rose from ₹231 crore in 1980–81 to ₹1,834 crore in 1990–91, almost ninefold!

Besides the above, the government of Prime Minister

V.P. Singh (1989–90), supported from the 'outside' by the BJP and the Communist Party of India (Marxist) (CPI[M]), engaged in some reckless populist actions, such as writing off ₹8,000 crores worth of loans due from farmers, raising procurement prices in crops twice in eleven months, thereby making net fiscal deficit of the government rise to 8.4 per cent of the GDP. Interest payments on internal debt rose from ₹1,369 crore in 1980–81 to ₹9,814 crore in 1990–91, more than sevenfold!

The combined effect of non-customable, non-commercial imports (fertilizers, petroleum, oil & lubricants [POL] and defence), interest payments of foreign debt and amortization of short-term debt, and decline in remittances created the balance of payments crisis. The balance of payments situation became so precarious that reserves came down to the level of about $1.3 billion, amounting to only about two weeks of imports, despite two International Monetary Fund (IMF) tranches of $2 billion. Inflation had also accelerated, reaching 16.7 per cent on an annual basis by August 1991. A drop in international confidence resulted in a sharp decline in capital inflow through commercial borrowings and non-resident deposits. In fact, capital flight began to take place. The record of high industrial and GDP growth experienced over the previous years thus came to naught by mid-1991.

A major concern during that period was the issue of promoting international competitiveness and improving India's share in world trade (which had declined from 2 per cent in 1951 to 0.4 per cent in 1990). The negative trade balance itself had widened during the 1980s, as Table 2 shows, while the CAD consistently rose from 1.7 per cent of GDP in 1980–81 to 3.3 per cent in 1989–90. India was hardly a participant when the world witnessed an unprecedented global trade boom between 1947 and 1975.

Table 2
India's Foreign Trade

(annual average/₹ in crore)

Period	Imports	Exports	Balance of trade
First Plan (1951–56)	735	605	−130
Second Plan (1956–61)	973	606	−367
Third Plan (1961–66)	1,240	753	−487
Annual Plan (1966–69)	1,998	1,238	−760
Fourth Plan (1969–74)	1,973	1,810	−163
Fifth Plan (1974–85)	5,220	4,479	−741
Sixth Plan (1980–85)	14,683	8,967	−5,716
Seventh Plan (1985–90)	25,152	17,482	−7,670

Source: Trade and Technology Directory of India, Government of India, 1991

In 1991 when the environment had hardened, it became necessary to harness foreign trade for survival. Naturally, unshackling of the Indian economy *became imperative.*

The question was how? The economy was in the quicksand of an inefficient, protected and high-cost industry that faced little competition. Or could it eventually face it and survive? This closed economy had led to the abandonment of comparative advantages in international trade. Hence, import control became mired in a vastly complicated system of licences and quantitative restrictions managed by an oversized bureaucracy. This, in turn, led to corruption and the rise of adventurer and pirate entrepreneurs, who further bled the system.

The corruption in the licences awarded generated 'black money' or unaccounted-for cash, which necessarily (to avoid detection) was spent on acquisition of luxury goods, five-star hotels and ostentatious wedding ceremonies. With a consequent increase in the demand for luxury goods, the higher profitability of industries producing these goods led to investments and imports being diverted and locked into this sector even more. Thus, based on Leontief's Input-Output Analysis, almost two-third of investments and imports was diverted to the production of 'non-wage' conspicuous consumption commodities, thoroughly defeating the purpose of the strict regime of import control and socialist planning itself. Exports also lost their competitiveness because the premium on imports was on its utilization in the luxury goods sector. Hence exports that required imports as essential inputs had to pay a high price for it. India's share in world trade, which was a mere 2 per cent in 1948, declined continuously to 0.5 per cent by 1980. Though there was a dilution in the strict import substitution policy in this period, a decline in the export competitiveness during the 1960s and 1970s meant that the non-Soviet Union hard currency exports did not rise to meet the higher import bill. This contributed to the financial and balance of payments crisis of 1991.

Table 3 further reinforces the fact that India had actually lost ground in rank internationally, in terms of per capita income, contribution of the manufacturing sector to GDP and exports. While India's position had improved in certain commodities, for which huge public-sector funds had been invested, this had not been enough to raise the country's position in the quality-of-life indicators, which remained low in international rank even amongst United Nations Economic and Social Commission for Asia and the Pacific (UNESCAP) countries. In fact, the 1990 United Nations Development Programme (UNDP's) Human Development Report brings out clearly that except for countries such as war-torn Afghanistan, India was at the near bottom of the list in terms of the Human Development Index.

Table 3
India's Ranking in the World (Select Indicators)

	1955	1989
Per capita GNP	105	161
Contribution of Mfg. sector to GDP	15	16
Cement	9	6
Crude steel	19	13
Machine tools	21	21
Passenger cars	13	21
Commercial vehicles	14	12
Electricity generated	22	11
Crude petroleum production	29	18
Coal production	4	5
Iron ore	8	6
Bauxite	15	10
Merchant vessels	21	13
Exports	19	47

Source: Based on World Development Reports, 1990; World Bank, 1990

Such a state of affairs even after decades of Independence was a matter of national shame and represented a graphic example of failure of the economic strategy that we had followed. It was thus an argument in itself for restructuring our economic policy, for the adoption of new objectives, fresh priorities and a relevant strategy, so that in the next three decades, we could be well within the reach of becoming a modern developed nation which could provide basic amenities to its people.

All these negative developments were compounded by two unexpected shocks: first was the collapse of the USSR-assured export market, which led to a slump in exports. The Soviet export market was wholly artificial, since India's exports, sold in rupees but at an overvalued rouble (of over twenty-eight times in 1980s), were re-exported by the USSR to hard currency areas. Since the Soviet Union played favourites with traders in India, this huge bleeding of Indian foreign exchange in opportunity cost is unparalleled in the world's modern plunder. Second, the First Gulf War that commenced with Iraq's annexation of Kuwait on 2 August 1990 caused a doubling of crude oil price and a freeze on Indian workers' remittance from West Asia. Our oil import bill rose sharply, doubling from $3 billion in 1988–89 to $6 billion in 1990–91. In rupee terms, it was even more due to rupee depreciation vis-à-vis the dollar. There was a run on NRI deposits due to panic, of ₹360 crore per week, in mid-1991. Between 1990–91 and 1991–92, deposits in NRI schemes dropped by ₹2,421 crore to ₹1,412 crore.

On top of it all, the Uruguay Round of talks on the new GATT and the WTO was reaching finalization (formalized in 1994), and the writing on the wall was clear: India's protectionist and captive economic environment had to end, and India had to make the transition to a globally competitive open market economic system by the twenty-first century.

This situation called for urgent action. International confidence had to be restored, inflation had to be brought under control, and the balance of payments had to be managed, so that the country could not only regain its pace of economic growth, but also raise it to new heights. The crisis had been caused by structural imbalances, which had built up over time. Therefore, structural reforms had to be undertaken simultaneously to strengthen the growth capability of the economy.

All these coincidental events made economic reform and liberalization inevitable. The Soviet economic model, thus, had its demise in India in early 1991. It was a matter of satisfaction to me that as a senior minister of the government in 1990–91, I could write its epitaph after having campaigned against the model for over two decades and, in the process, suffering ostracization in India's academia and the denial of the opportunity to teach as a professor.

The Five Pillars of Transformation

The case for restructuring the Indian economic policy in 1991 thus rested on five major premises.

First, the erroneous adoption of the Soviet model through our Five-Year Plans had produced distortions, imbalances and mismatches leading to inflation, perpetuation of poverty, unemployment and low quality of life. The time had come to discard the model, and adopt another one that was consistent with our national objectives and priorities, so that India could become a front-rank country internationally.

Second, the agricultural sector had to be modernized and diversified to be able to produce surpluses over domestic demand to make exports of agricultural processed products possible. India had already become a large producer of food products, as Table 4 will show, and with infrastructural support, it had become a leading exporter. The agricultural sector needed to be developed to absorb the labour force in the sector to reduce the pressure on urban centres and maintain a higher quality of life.

Table 4
Production of Food Products and India's Ranking in the World

	World Total (M.T.)	India (M.T.)	India's Ranking in the World
Rice (paddy)	535	118	2
Wheat	528	59	3
Groundnut (shell)	28.5	8.4	2
Cotton	18.4	2.3	3
Tobacco	6.5	0.5	3
Tea	2.6	0.7	1
Potatoes	265	15.00	6
Milk (cow and buffalo)	506.8	61.2	2
Butter and ghee	6.7	1.2	1
Eggs (hen)	39.4	1.5	5
Sugar	11.00	10.6	2

Source: *World Food Output*, Food and Agriculture Organization, UN, Rome, 1992

Note: M.T.=Million Tonnes

Third, if India was to maintain its independence, it had to encourage its industry to become cost-conscious to be internationally competitive. Industrial output had to meet acceptable quality levels to be exportable, and be price-attractive without subsidization.

Fourth, the allocation of resources had to be made more efficient so that India was able to achieve a higher growth rate, with the existing level of national savings. For this, new forms of ownership, including privatization, to induce greater accountability in public- and private-sector corporations, had to be adopted.

Fifth, it was important to carry out fiscal reforms to mobilize resources from new and untapped areas, and reduce the tax burden on the common man. These fiscal reforms had to steer the country clear of the two debt traps, fiscal and foreign exchange, that lay close ahead.

It was clear that the investment policy, followed during the entire Soviet model plan period (1952–91), was not according to the above five premises, and hence required a complete reflection, which began in 1991.

5

A TRYST WITH DESTINY THAT NEVER MATERIALIZED

In the early 1990s, after jettisoning the Soviet model in Indian planning, there was a dream of India becoming a 'new tiger'—a fast-growing economy on the 'East Asia pattern', with the hope that poverty and unemployment would be wiped out in just one decade of GDP growth (at 10 per cent per year). Towards that objective, after the 1990–91 Balance of Payment crisis, as the commerce minister, I suggested an economic reform package designed to deal with two issues:

a) In the short term, to stabilize the foreign exchange situation by inducting $2 billion, obtained from the IMF as a loan on the concessional interest rate, into the reserves.

b) In the medium term, to restructure the economy so that it could move to a high growth path, through exports and discharge the foreign exchange debt to a manageable level.

The crisis was tackled decisively, thanks to the US assisting us in getting a $2 billion condition-free loan from the IMF. This became possible because of two reasons. First, I had prevailed on Prime Minister Chandra Shekhar to allow US Air Force planes, flying from the Philippines Air Force Base to Saudi Arabia for the Gulf War, to refuel in Chennai, Mumbai, Nagpur and Agra. The US was very pleased by this gesture, which led to a dramatic change in its attitude towards our country. As a consequence, the IMF granted a special $2 billion loan on concessional terms, and thus India overcame the debt-repayment default. Second, the exchange rate was adjusted to realistic levels, to reduce the need for export subsidies, which was a pressure on budgetary resources. This was accompanied by major changes in trade policy. Most of these measures had been prepared in a document by me as the commerce minister. The Chandra Shekhar Cabinet approved these trade reform plans on 11 March 1991. After this tackling of the fire ignited by the previous V.P. Singh government's recklessness, the steps taken by the succeeding Rao government (in which I held a Cabinet rank post) was successful in restoring international confidence and improving the foreign exchange situation. My trade reform proposals became the basis for a comprehensive deregulation liberalization soon after, in 1992.

With the restoration of external confidence and the beginning of efforts to control the fiscal deficit, the medium-term steps to restore growth and productivity were taken in late 1991; a major effort was made to deregulate the individual and foreign trade sectors so that industrialists and entrepreneurs could take their own decisions on what and how to produce, subject only to certain minimum restrictions, e.g. its effect on the environment. In the fertilizer sector, for example, entry was now free, but regulations over price and distribution remained indirect instruments of control over private investment. The government still fixed consumer prices, and ex-factory prices for each plant in the country, and approved the technology and equipment used for any expansion. Even though private investment had been deregulated, the government, however, still had discretion to determine its financial viability.

After the fairly wide-ranging reforms initiated in 1991–93, the GDP accelerated from the annual growth rate slump of 0.8 per cent in 1990–91 to 7.8 per cent in 1996–97. In the 1992–97 phase (Eighth Plan), a sustained growth of over 7 per cent, which was double the rate of the previous forty-one years (i.e. the 1950–91 period), naturally raised the country's hopes of achieving an even higher growth rate of 10+ per cent in the new millennium. This has not yet been realized. The higher growth rate in the 1990s, however, was achieved, unlike after Rajiv Gandhi's minimal deregulation in foreign trade and investment in the 1980s, and without the balance of payment crisis we had witnessed in 1990–91. On the contrary, during 1991–98, the foreign exchange reserves rose to $32 billion, which was about eight months of the annual import bill, and far from the near default syndrome of 1990–91, which was due to the disastrous tenure of V.P. Singh as the prime minister (1989–90). However, this steady encouraging trend did not last beyond the early 2000s. The GDP growth rate dropped over the next two decades (2004–14). What went wrong?

Clearly, despite the openly declared commitment to economic reforms, the road to India becoming a competitive global economy still has many speed breakers. The Congress party (of which Prime Minister Rao was also the president during 1991–96) never came to terms with the question of market economy reforms in good conscience. This was because Rao's senior ministers, including Arjun Singh, N.D. Tiwari and K. Karunakaran, never supported him and were hardcore socialists believing in command economy as the salvation. The Congress formally split in 1995 into the

Congress and Congress (Tiwari), unable to reconcile reformists and reactionaries.

The Rao government, in order to minimize the opposition in the Congress party, treated the reform movement's deviating from socialist ideology as a necessary but 'temporary evil'. It pained the party leaders to recognize reforms as an abandonment of what Nehru had preached for decades, brainwashing many. Because the party failed to reconcile with the reforms ideologically, the Congress party failed to move in unison with the basic direction of the economic reform and thus split as mentioned earlier. The Eighth Five-Year Plan is the most outstanding example of the left hand of a government being unaware of what the right hand was up to. The Plan envisaged an average annual growth rate target of 5.6, but the Rao government had achieved nearly 7 per cent annual growth rate before that, in the mid-Plan period itself! This was something (the actual growth rate in the GDP being more than the planned growth rate) that had never happened since 1950, until 1994.

Obviously, to begin with, the movement towards a market economy through economic reforms cannot be consistent with a Five-Year Plan, which requires the state to absorb 70–80 per cent of the household savings and deploy it as planned expenditure. The choice is always between the reforms being scuttled and the centralized plans being scrapped. Both cannot coexist. But the Congress party never did clearly declare its commitment—a market economy or state-directed planning. As per the new series of National Accounts (Base 1993–94), the service sector accounted for as much as 50.1 per cent of the GDP from 1993–94 to 1998–99. The compositional (share in GDP) shift in favour of services has been brought about by accelerated expansion in the service sector output at a rate of 8.4 per cent in the period 1992–93 to 1997–98, as compared with 6.5 per cent during 1980–91 to 1990–91. The service sector is largely unregulated by the state and is driven by the private sector.

But it was not just the Congress party that was hesitant to make a decisive break with the past. In fact, the hopes raised by the reforms initiated during the tenures of Chandra Shekhar (1990–91) and Narasimha Rao (1991–96) dimmed with the advent of the new millennium under the Vajpayee-led National Democratic Alliance (NDA) (1998–2004). In the 'second generation', most of the structural reforms were further delayed and diluted by the Vajpayee government, since it was a coalition of ideologically different parties. From 2004 till 2014, the Congress-dominated UPA was driven by special interest groups, i.e. the rent-earning losers mostly from Rao-driven deregulation. These were people who got used to captive markets, protectionist policies and the government's directives, and made money by selling subsidized, licenced and quota-based raw materials and intermediate products to the private sector in the black market.

As a consequence, industrial growth decelerated during the second half of the first decade of the twenty-first century. Export growth fell in early 2000, and struggled till 2018–19 to recover to the 1992–96 growth rate level. Infrastructure bottlenecks have now become a major obstacle to growth in the economy, while agriculture today exhibits massive instability and fluctuation in growth rates. From 1998–99 till 2014, the GDP growth rate marginally increased to 6 per cent, hampered due to a declining growth rate in the manufacturing and service sectors. Industrial growth decelerated even more sharply from a peak of 13.2 per cent in 2004 to below 3 per cent by the mid-second decade i.e., 2014. Gross Domestic Capital Formation (GDCF) growth slowed down; gross fiscal deficit, for Centre and states put together—legally mandated not to exceed 3 per cent under the Fiscal Management Act of Parliament—rose to 8.5 per cent of the GDP!

The economic reforms were more in the nature of relaxing and easing the remaining controls and shackles, and not of scrapping them and replacing with structural reforms. Naturally, there is today much concern nationally about the 'reversibility' of reforms, and the consequent reluctance of foreign technology-laden foreign direct investment (FDI) to pour into the country into long gestation investments. The required extent of such FDI that is essential for accelerating the growth rate of GDP can only be realistically expected when there is investor confidence that policies for market reform and liberation are framed with a stable political commitment. Unfortunately for India, the stewardship of the Ministry of Finance displayed a level of erratic trends in tax, investment and uncertainty, thus dampening the initial enthusiasm of foreign investors. This is reflected even in the trends, since 2014, in technology-laden FDI during the BJP government.

Significant Structural Change

The experience of the 1990s shows that there had indeed been a marked structural transformation of the economy. The inter-sectoral composition of the GDP underwent a significant change after the initiation of the reform process. The relative share of 'agriculture and allied activities' in the GDP during the period 1992–93 to 1997–98 declined to 17.5 per cent from 24.5 per cent during the period 1980–81 to 1990–91. On the other hand, the share of industry increased from 23.2 per cent to 25.9 per cent and that of the service sector (including construction) moved up substantially from 42.2 per cent to 46.6 per cent in the same period.

The poor and erratic performance of agriculture, especially in food crops and animal husbandry, was partly due to the petering out of the Green Revolution, since the acreage brought under high-yielding varieties (HYVs) and irrigation had slowed in the 1990s. This is attributed to the consistent neglect in the allocation of public investment to this sector, as shown in Table 1. Even the allocated amount of a mere 8 per cent of the public investment was not fully spent in the Eighth Plan and more than 40 per cent of it was unspent. Since agriculture is basically a private sector of a large number of poor cultivators, public investment has a critical role to play in creating infrastructure, roads and markets, besides facilitating education and healthcare for the rural people. That responsibility is of the government, which abdicated its duty to agriculture despite wide-ranging reforms in other sectors (during 1992–97).

Table 1
Planned and Actual Sectoral Public Investment 1992–97

(₹crore at 1996–97 prices)

Sector	Planned	Actual	Per Cent of Planned
Agriculture	64.9	38.3	59
Secondary	244.9	219.0	89
Tertiary	190.2	203.0	107
Total	500	460.3	92

Source: *Ninth Five-Year Plan*, Planning Commission, GOI quoted in R. Thamaralakshi, 'Agriculture and Economic Reform', *Economic & Political Weekly*, 14 August 1999

The relative deceleration in the performance of agriculture during the 1990s (see tables 2 and 3) clearly indicates that favourable monsoons, increase in net irrigated area and positive terms of trade did not have the desired impact. The decline in public investment (see tables 4 and 5) and the limited infusion of new technologies instead seem to have defined the decline.

Table 2
Foodgrain Production (1995–2000)

(Million Tonnes)

Crop	1995–96	1996–97	1997–98	1998–99	1999–2000
Rice	77.0	81.7	82.5	86.0	87.5
Wheat	62.1	69.4	66.3	70.8	68.7
Coarse Cereals	29.0	34.1	30.4	31.5	29.2
Pulses	12.3	14.2	12.0	14.8	13.5
Foodgrains	180.4	199.4	192.3	203.0	199.1
Rabi	85.3	95.5	90.7	99.7	95.9

Source: Data collected by the author from statistical abstracts published by Ministry of Agriculture, Government of India

Table 3
Commercial Crop Production (1995–2000)

(Million Tonnes)

Crop	1995–96	1996–97	1997–98	1998–99	1999–2000 @
Groundnut	7.6	8.6	7.4	9.2	5.8
Rapeseed/Mustard	6.0	6.7	4.7	5.8	6.1
Soya Bean	5.1	5.4	6.5	6.9	6.5
Other Six Oilseeds	3.4	3.7	2.8	3.3	3.1
Total Nine Oilseeds	22.1	24.4	21.3	25.2	21.6
Cotton*	12.9	14.2	10.9	12.2	12.1
Jute and Mesta**	8.8	11.1	11.0	9.7	10.6
Sugarcane	281.1	277.6	279.5	295.7	315.1

Source: Data collected by the author from statistical abstracts published by Ministry of Agriculture, Government of India

*Million bales of 170 kg each, **Million bales of 180 kg each, @Estimated

Table 4

Gross Capital Formation

Average for Each Period at Constant (1980–81) Prices

(Price, ₹Crore)

	Agriculture	Secondary	Tertiary	Total
1985–91	4342	20970	17150	42462
	(10.2)	(49.4)	(40.4)	(100.0)
1991–97	5891	31384	24831	62106
	(9.5)	(50.5)	(40.4)	(100.0)

Source: Table assembled from National Income, Central Statistics Office (CSO), 2000

Note: Figures in brackets are percentages to total

Table 5

Gross Capital Formation in Public and Private Sectors

Average for Each Period at Constant (1980–81)

(Price, ₹Crore)

	Agriculture	Non-Agriculture	Total
Public Sector	11347	18229	19576
1985–91	(6.9)	(93.1)	(100.0)
1991–97	1155	21020	22175
	(5.2)	(94.8)	(100.0)
Private Sector	2995	19891	22886
1985–91	(13.1)	(86.9)	(100.0)
1991–97	4736	35195	39931
	(11.9)	(88.1)	(100.0)

Source: Central Statistics Office (CSO), op. cit.

Note: Figures in brackets are percentages to total

As per World Bank estimates, Total Factor Productivity (TFP) growth was negative in agriculture in the first half of the 1990s. TFP measures the multiplier effect on growth due to productivity in the use of capital and labour and moving from a production curve to a higher curve and not along the same curve that tapers off due to the law of diminishing returns.

While it is clear that the inconsistent performance in agriculture during the period of reforms (1992–93) was due to the consistent neglect of the sector (which has been the case since 1973–74) in terms of public investment, trade, bank credit and market access, it is equally important to understand the factors leading to the deceleration in the structural performance of the industrial sector.

There are several reasons that can be attributed for the fall in industrial growth.

i) Deceleration in industrial investment

Gross fixed capital formation (GFCF) grew in 1994–95 at 11.3 per cent and at 18.9 per cent in 1995–96, and then fell to 6.3 per cent (1996–97) and further declined to 5.2 per cent in 1997–98.

ii) Poor performance of agriculture

This meant that demand as well as purchasing power of rural consumers were low. This was a major factor in scaling down industrial expansion, which was hit by poor demand for industrial products.

iii) Bank credit and loans became more difficult

Due to the rise in detection of bank frauds, managers became more risk-averting and conservative, which made banks hunt for very low-risk projects and government securities (Table 6).

Table 6

Gross Rates of Bank Credit

	Gross Bank Credit	Non-Food Credit	Industrial Credit (in per cent)
1993–96 (annual average)	18.2	18.4	21.6
1996–97	9.6	10.9	10.8
1997–98	16.4	15.1	15.5
April–October			
1997–98	1.9	0.3	–1.1
1998–99	4.2	2.9	2.0

Source: 'Survey of Industry', *The Hindu*, 1999

As a result, the flow of bank credit to the industry declined during 1996–97. But banks ought not to be afraid of vigilance being strictly adhered to in public interest. Unfortunately, public-sector banks (PSBs) with politicians on the boards have always treated loan-advancing as patronage and not as something impersonal to be decided on merit. This is apparent in 2019 in the form of the high percentage of non-performing assets (NPAs). Even privatization of banks will not help the situation, as private banks are not significantly free of corrupt practices.

iv) Infrastructural bottlenecks

During 1992–95, infrastructural sectors grew more rapidly than before, at over 8 per cent per year, but thereafter it decelerated sharply to 2 per cent, mainly due to decline in steel, coal, oil and freight movement.

v) WTO-induced lower-cost imports and tariff reduction

As part of the nation's commitments to the new GATT (1995), quotas (quantitative restrictions [QRs]) had to be abolished, and tariffs progressively reduced. The average tariff on imports was reduced from 138 per cent ad valorem to 55 per cent, and brought down further to below 40 per cent by 31 March 2001. This meant that the progressively cheaper imports faced competitive challenge from domestically produced, high-cost industrial products. The then government (UPA) made no serious effort to promote exports that were faced with a seriously declining growth rate due to this factor. Furthermore, whatever growth in exports was achieved was from gems, garments, rice, tea and coffee—hardly a basket for an industrializing country. Of course, software was also picking up. The need of the hour for the government was to cut the cost of capital to a level that foreign enterprises paid for in their own countries. This would have significantly reduced the challenge, faced by domestic industry, to the flood of imports in the new millennium.

An important feature of the growth process in the 1990s was, fortunately, the continued dominance of the service sector as an important contributor to the overall growth of the economy. In the 1980s and 1990s, the growth in this sector continued at a steadily increasing level. The average annual growth of the service sector had increased from 6.6 per cent during 1981–90 to 7.1 per cent during 1990–98. Following the general trend in other sectors, there was a slight deceleration in the growth of this sector in 1996–97 too, although the annual growth rate still remained way above that of the manufacturing and agricultural sectors. In terms of composition, barring real estate, most other industries in the service sector had experienced a steady growth in the 1990s. In the case of the construction sector, there had been a turnaround, with annual growth rates increasing from 0.94 per cent in 1993–94 to 9.72 per cent in 1996–97, while the growth in real estate remained low, around 3 per cent throughout the 1990s. The deceleration in the growth of the service sector since 1996–97 was driven by the slowdown in the growth of finance and banking, trade and real estate. The complete foreign trade data for the entire period since Independence (1949–50) to the beginning of the twenty-first century (1999–2000) is presented in Table 7 for a complete perspective.

It was expected that economic reforms would lead to an increase in exports and improve trade balance. In spite of the depreciation of the rupee rate, imports continued to rise rapidly. Trade deficits increased from $1,546 million in 1991–92 to $8,199 million in 1998–99. In the growth of output, even during an upturn in 1999–2000, the agriculture export rate continued to be negative. While the share of agriculture and allied products in total export declined sharply during the 1980s, the share of gems and jewellery rose during the same period. Exports of chemical and allied products grew constantly during the 1980s and 1990s. Exports of manufactures increased because of a rapid increase in software exports, which grew from $225 million in 1992–93 to $2,650 million in 1998–99. However, except software, no new export industry developed in the 1990s. Global exports recorded only a modest 4 per cent growth in volume terms in 1998, against a 10 per cent rise in the previous year.

The upshot of all these voluminous data is that economic reform, while domestically had led to acceleration in the GDP growth, the foreign sector, i.e. export-import trade, had not benefitted due to the failure to fully implement the proposals I had made as the commerce minister, which had been adopted by the Cabinet on 11 March 1991.

Table 7
Exports, Imports and Trade Balance

(US $ Million)

Year	Exports (including re-exports)	Imports	Trade Balance	Rate of Change Exports (per cent)	Rate of Change Imports (per cent)
1	2	3	4	5	6
1949–50	1016	1292	–276		
1950–51	1269	1273	–4	24.9	–1.5
1951–52	1490	1852	–362	17.4	45.5
1952–53	1212	1472	–260	–18.6	–20.5
1953–54	1114	1279	–166	–8.1	–13.1
1954–55	1233	1456	–233	10.7	13.8
1955–56	1275	1620	–345	3.3	11.3
1956–57	1259	1750	–491	1.2	8.0
1957–58	1171	2160	–989	–7.0	23.4
1958–59	1219	1901	–682	4.2	–12.0
1959–60	1343	2016	–674	10.1	6.0
1961–62	1381	2281	–900	2.6	–3.1
1962–63	1437	2372	–935	4.0	4.0
1963–64	1659	2558	–899	15.5	7.8
1964–65	1701	2813	–1111	2.6	10.0
1965–66	1693	2944	–1251	–0.5	4.7
1966–67	1628	2923	–1295	–3.9	–0.7
1967–68	1586	2656	–1071	–2.6	–9.1
1968–69	1788	2513	–726	12.7	–5.4
1969–70	1866	2089	–223	4.4	–16.9
1970–71	2031	2162	–131	8.8	3.5
1971–72	2153	2443	–290	6.0	13.0
1972–73	2550	2415	134	18.4	–1.1
1973–74	3209	3759	–549	25.9	55.6

1974–75	4175	5666	−1492	30.1	50.8
1975–76	4665	6084	−1420	11.7	7.4
1976–77	5753	5677	77	23.3	−6.7
1977–78	6316	7031	−715	9.8	23.9
1978–79	6978	8300	−1322	10.5	18.0
1979–80	7947	11321	−3374	13.9	36.4
1980–81	7486	15869	−7383	6.8	40.2
1981–82	8704	15174	−6470	2.6	−4.4
1982–83	9107	14787	−5679	4.6	2.6
1983–84	9449	15311	−5861	3.8	3.5
1984–85	9878	14412	−4534	4.5	−5.9
1985–86	8904	16067	−7162	−9.9	11.5
1986–87	9745	15727	−5982	9.4	−2.1
1987–88	12089	17156	−5067	24.1	9.1
1988–89	13970	19497	−5526	15.6	13.6
1989–90	16612	21219	−4607	18.9	8.8
1990–91	18143	24075	−5932	9.2	13.5
1991–92	17865	19411	1546	−1.5	−19.4
1992–93	18537	21882	−3345	3.8	12.7
1993–94	22238	23306	−1068	20.0	6.5
1994–95	26330	28654	−2324	18.4	22.9
1995–96	31797	36678	−4881	20.8	28.0
1996–97	33470	39133	−5663	5.3	6.7
1997–98	35006	41484	−6478	4.6	6.0
1998–99 (P)	33659	41858	−8199	−3.9	0.9
1999–2000 (P) (Apr–Dec)	27419	34458	−7039	12.9	9.0

Source: Economic Survey, 2000–01, Ministry of Finance, 27 February 2000

Notes: P: Provisional; For the years 1956–57, 1957–58, 1958–59 and 1959–60, the data are as per the Fourteenth Report of the Estimates Committee (1971–72) of the erstwhile Ministry of Foreign Trade

The reform process had demanded a basic shift in the investment policy, in the structure of decision-making for efficient allocation of resources. We needed to shift from the centralized hybrid 'command' economy of the 1980s, to a system in which decisions were made by economic units freely, subject to the certain but few parameters of a national social welfare policy adopted by the Parliament. In such an economy, private enterprise was allowed freedom within the parameters of social justice. This called for the privatization of the Indian economy, but coupled with concern for the poor, through a 'safety net' for them.

At that point in time, investments in the private organized sector were approximately ₹75,000 crore; the investment in Central and state PSUs was in excess of ₹1,30,000 crore. If to this we added the investment in departmental undertakings such as the Railways and P&T, the total investment by the Centre and state undertakings was in excess of ₹3,00,000 crore. The return on this massive investment in PSUs was less than 1 per cent—a criminal waste of resources due to socialist cronyism, remnants of which were entrenched in the public sector.

By contrast, the return in the organized private sector on an average was around 10 per cent. In fact, if one were to compare industry-wise, e.g., power, fertilizers, hotels, heavy engineering, etc., the private sector outperformed the public sector. This fact alone recommended selective privatization as a measure for achieving efficiency.

As per rigorous economic analysis as a rule-of-the-thumb measure, a simple back-of-the-envelope calculation of the difference between dividends plus interest (receipt from PSUs) and the shadow price of government investment evaluated by multiplying equity plus loans plus working capital by 9.6 per cent (opportunity cost) showed that PSUs in 1994–95 received ₹4,667 crore as subsidies. Much was made of agricultural and public distribution system (PDS) subsidies, but the subsidization of PSUs was hardly referred to in any discussion, nor reflected in the Budget, since it was implicit.

In fact, wherever the government has encouraged the private sector instead of a public sector, unless national interest requires it to be maintained, as in the case of Air India, positive results have emanated. In agriculture, for example, the Green Revolution in India had been founded on the private ownership of the means of production, with the help of the government's R&D assistance. The easing of the foreign exchange crisis in India during the 1970s and 1980s was due to the private initiative of our skilled and semi-skilled labour, which temporarily migrated to the Gulf region in search of jobs. Later, from 1990 till date, it is the software electronics-skilled labour force that has boosted the nation's foreign exchange reserves. It all began with the outsourcing of paperwork and the typing of documents transmitted through the Internet. But the software revolution in India was entirely a private-sector initiative assisted by the state.

In other words, the lesson to be drawn is that if the government helps the private sector to flourish, it will actually boom! That is the meaning of 'market economy' and the role of the state.

The government was unable to do the same with PSUs. Of the 242 Central PSUs, only twenty were profit-makers, and that too because of administered prices. More than a hundred were explicit loss-makers, of which forty-eight were chronically sick, with their equity fully eroded. Considering that government bonds yielded 12 per cent and commercial bank loans fetched 18 per cent, and also taking into account the fact that PSUs acquired land through the government, received subsidy on commercial loans and had assured markets, the performance of India's public sector was dismal. The huge squandering of public resources the PSUs represented was a criminal breach of the people's trust.

The main reason for the poor performance of PSUs was the lack of accountability. Since share capital of the PSUs was wholly owned by the government, there was no one to question the management. Internal accountability was zero or rigged. The Parliament is empowered to audit through the Public Accounts Committee (PAC) and public undertaking committees, but the workload of the MPs and the general qualification of those elected (to grasp fine financial fudging of data) being what it is, there is just no overseeing at all of the PSUs. The situation is much worse at the state level, where the accounts of many state-owned PSUs have not been audited for more than five years.

This lack of accountability in PSUs began right from the project stage. Cost and time overruns in the completion of public-sector projects were extensive. According to a study of the 290 projects (of cost over ₹20 crore) under implementation as of 31 March 1987,[21] 186 had cost overruns, while 162 had time overruns. Further, the cost overruns were as much as 50 per cent, while time overruns were 43 per cent. As a consequence, the nation lost about ₹20,000 crore in overruns. By 1999, the situation had not much improved.

At the end of September 1999, of the total of 201 projects, 103 were delayed, which accounted for 51.2 per cent of the total Central-sector projects. The railways had the largest number of delayed projects (twenty-one), followed closely by petroleum (nineteen), power (sixteen), surface transport (sixteen) and coal (fifteen). Together, these five sectors accounted for over 84.5 per cent of the total delayed projects. There were fifty-four projects without a date of commissioning. The railways

---

[21]Sebastian Morris, 'Cost and Time Overruns in Public Sector Projects', *Economic & Political Weekly*, Vol. 25, No. 47, pp. M154–M168, 24 November 1990

had the largest number of projects (fifty-two) without a date of commissioning. An analysis of year-wise distribution of delayed projects showed that at the end of September 1999, out of 103 projects, (i) Forty-two were delayed by two to five years; (ii) Twenty-eight were delayed by up to one year; (iii) Seventeen were delayed by five to ten years; and (iv) Sixteen were delayed by one to two years.

Going by the reasons for the delay in the projects, it was found that the maximum number of projects (twenty) were delayed due to problems in civil works. Sixteen projects were affected due to problems in equipment supply, followed by fourteen projects due to the problem of land. Problems of funds and the awarding of contracts affected thirteen projects each.

The magnitude of cost overrun in respect of delayed projects was 65.7 per cent over the original cost for the relevant projects in September 1999. Sector-wise, power, atomic energy, steel and railways accounted for around 84.3 per cent of the cost escalation. The cost had more than doubled in atomic energy, finance and power projects.

Considering that the share of public saving in total saving was about 8 per cent, while its share in total investment was nearly 60 per cent, the need of the hour was to put a stop to this gigantic draining of our resources. This lopsided guzzling of resources and bureaucratization were highlighted by the fact that 60 per cent of the paper output in the country was consumed in government activities. Much of the paperwork of the government had become redundant and was found to be setting an obstacle course for investors. It was easier and more rewarding in such a maze of regulations to be risk-averters for managers, when, instead, the requirement was to be risk-takers in order to be innovative. In any case, the heads of public-sector corporations tended to be from the bureaucracy, who regarded such positions to be either demotions or transit stops. It was too much to expect them to be dynamic risk-takers in such an environment.

Thus, within the decade of 1990s, we could have achieved a much higher growth in GDP and at a much lower cost by a proper restructuring of the investment pattern. The nation has been fortunate in having such a high rate of domestic saving (32 per cent of GDP), but this is not due to the efforts of the government. On the contrary, public-sector saving consistently declined from 3.7 per cent of the GDP during the Sixth Plan (it was 4.6 per cent in 1981–82) to a mere 0.6 per cent of the GDP in 1989–90. The picture was even more dismal in case of government-saving. As a ratio of the GDP, the government-saving declined from minus 1.9 per cent in 1984–85 to a deeper minus of 3.8 per cent in 1989–90. This was an unacceptable state of affairs—a government whose financial hold on the economy was near total, had become such a guzzler of resources and yet was not accountable for it in any concrete way. We needed to therefore consider restructuring the role of the public sector in general and that of the government in particular, to ensure accountability and achieve efficient utilization of resources and a better economic performance.

The continued blind emphasis on the public sector has thus produced dissatisfaction. There is a growing consensus in India that the bureaucracy cannot manage these enterprises, and the mismanagement of the last three decades has resulted in inefficiency and a squandering of resources. This consensus has a sound empirical basis. A comparison of financial ratios to assess the performance of the public sector vis-à-vis the private sector provides a vivid contrast. Consider, for example, the net profit, after taxes, as a ratio of the capital employed. Even in the public sector's best year (1981–82), this ratio (a good measure of the rate of profitability) for the public sector was only half that of the private sector. It may be argued that the public sector does not aim to make profits and that its goal is to add to production. According to the ratio of value added to capital employed, the private sector shows a far superior performance. The ratio for the public sector is just 0.356, while it is 0.492 for the private sector. And the gap between public- and private-sector performance is even wider if you take into account the fact that the public sector gets a number of advantages that are denied to the private sector. For example, loans to the private sector are at 12–18 per cent interest, while banks are forced to buy government securities. Property is acquired more easily for the public sector and at lower rates of compensation. Moreover, if just three enterprises—the State Trading Corporation (STC), the Minerals and Metals Trading Corporation (MMTC) and the Oil and Natural Gas Commission (ONGC)—are excluded from the public sector, the gap in the performance of the public and private sectors becomes amazingly wide.

Even in the matter of financing, the private sector in India is more self-reliant. The component of investment, which is measured by the GFCF, and financed by the internal resources of the enterprise, is 81 per cent for the private sector and just 26 per cent for the public sector.

Protagonists of the public sector cannot produce even one criterion by which their sector can be shown to be superior to the private sector in performance. One sometimes hears that the public sector cannot be compared to the private sector because, in the former, the investments have long gestation lags, whereas the private-sector-investment portfolio consists of 'quickies'. Wrong again. If one considers any set of performance criteria for the same product with the same gestation lags—the public sector Steel Authority of India Limited (SAIL) and the private sector Tata Iron and Steel Company Limited (TISCO) or similarly, that of the Fertilizer Corporation of India (FCI) with Coromandel International Limited or even Heavy Engineering Corporation (HEC) with Utkal Machinery Private Limited (UML)—the private sector comes out on top again. And remember that the price for the output is set by the public sector. Even in matters of R&D, innovation, patents and social welfare, the private sector is ahead in actual performance.

Therefore, we must accept the fact that the bureaucracy cannot manage an enterprise and that, wherever feasible and in public interest, the process of privatization should be initiated to achieve greater efficiency and performance.

The experience of the last forty years of planned economic development shows that the organized sector has increasingly failed to provide adequate employment opportunities to a growing educated population. In the year 2011, unemployment levels were high, probably around 14 per cent of the 375 million-strong skilled and semi-skilled labour force. The number of persons registered with the largely urban-located Employment Exchanges was about 35 million. The organized sector provided only 28 million jobs—20 million in the public sector and 8 million in the private sector—which was about 8 per cent of the labour force.

The high rate of population growth in the last two decades has resulted in higher incidence of unemployment. Between 1994 and 1997, the population grew by 1.85 per cent annually to reach 950 million in April 1997 (see Table 8). But the employable population of the country grew at the rate of 2.27 per cent a year in the same time to reach 397 million in 1997.[22]

---

[22]Saibal Das Gupta, 'Employable Population Swells to 397m', *Business Standard*, 27 January 2013

Table 8
Population and Labour Force Growth

	Population millions % growth		Labour Force millions % growth		Labour Participation [(3) as % of (1)]
	1	2	3	4	5
1978	637.2	–	255.8	–	40.12
1983	718.2	2.16	286.6	2.07	39.91
1994	895.0	2.10	368.5	2.39	41.17
1997	951.2	1.85	397.2	2.27	41.76
2002	1028.9	1.57	449.6	2.48	43.70
2007 Projection	1112.9	1.57	507.9	2.44	45.64
2012	1196.4	1.45	562.9	2.06	47.05

Source: Ninth Five-Year Plan (1997–2000), Planning Commission, New Delhi, April

Employment opportunities also grew faster during 1994–97. The employment growth rate was 2.47 per cent a year between 1994 and 1997 as compared to 2.31 per cent during the period 1983–84, according to the Ninth Plan document. During the period of economic reform, there was clearly a discernible decline in the growth of employment in the organized sectors, especially in the public sector. Interestingly, two-third of this employment growth was in agriculture. But this growth in employment opportunities failed to keep pace with the demand from new additions to the labour force. This is understandable, but the social consequences have to be mitigated, which of late has got superficial attention from all governments. The National Renewal Fund (NRF) was instituted in 1992 for this purpose, but has remained dormant.

The National Sample Survey Office (NSSO) survey (43rd Round) on employment and dimensions of economic reforms since 1991 revealed that during the ten-year period ending 1997–98, employment had grown at about 1 per cent per annum, as can be inferred from Table 9. This growth, which had been about half the rate of growth of the labour force, had thus not been able to absorb the backlog of unemployment (of about 10.8 million) that existed in 1977–78, and remained undiminished till 1998.

Table 9
Dimensions of Economic Reforms Since 1991

Growth Rates of Employment in the Organized Sector (per cent)			
Year	Public Sector	Private Sector	Total Organized
1991	1.52	1.24	1.44
1992	0.80	2.21	1.21
1993	0.60	0.06	0.44
1994	0.62	1.01	0.73
1995	0.11	1.63	0.55
1996	(–) 0.19	5.62	1.51
1997	0.67	2.01	1.09
1998	(–) 0.09	1.72	0.46

Source: Planning Commission, Ninth Plan Documents, 1998

Therefore, the Eighth Five-Year Plan (1992–97) aimed at bringing employment into sharper focus in a mid-term perspective with the goal of reducing unemployment to a negligible proportion by 2002. It estimated that the employment potential would grow at about 2.6 per cent per annum during 1992–97. The plan envisaged the creation of additional employment opportunities of the order of 8.5 million per annum on an average during the Plan period and of the order of 9.5 million per annum on an average during the period 1997–2002 (see Table 10).

Table 10

Population and Labour Force: 1997–2002 (in Million)

Year	Population	Five-yearly increase	Labour force	Five-yearly increase	Labour force participation rate
1997	951.18		397.22		41.76
2002	1,028.93	77.75	449.62	52.40	43.69
2007	1,112.86	83.93	507.94	58.32	45.64
2012	1,196.41	83.55	562.91	54.97	47.05
Growth Rates					
1997–2002	1.58		2.51		
2002–07	1.58		2.47		
2007–12	1.46		2.07		

Source: Compiled and computed from the data given in the Ninth Five-Year Plan (1997–2002), Vol. I by Ruddar Datt, 'Arithmetic of Employment Growth', Youth Indian, 17 April 1999

About 18.8 million additional job opportunities were indeed generated during the post-reform period (1992–93 to 1994–95). Nearly half (9.03 million) of these had been in agriculture and allied sectors alone, which paradoxically were not included in the reform schemes. The manufacturing sector, which should have led the employment spurt, came third in employment generation (3 million), even after the trade and transport sector. It is obvious now in retrospect that the programmes were not properly designed, and thus led to the slowing down of employment growth, causing the reforms themselves to become unpopular.

By the end of the Ninth Plan (1997–2002), the labour force growth—because of increased life expectancy—reached a peak level of 2.51 per cent per annum—the highest it has ever been.

The Ninth Plan had prepared estimates of the elasticity of employment. Employment elasticity for the economy as a whole was 0.40 during the decade 1983 to 1993–94. It was likely to show a marginal decline to 0.38 during the Ninth Plan, owing to a decline in the employment elasticity of manufacturing from 0.33 to 0.25 and of finance, real estate, and insurance and business services from 0.90 to 0.53.

Unemployment thus continues to remain a serious problem. As usual, the government claims that the situation was alarming but attributable to rapid population growth and induction of new technologies. This cannot be true because population growth has tapered (since 1991) from 2.5 per cent in the 1960s to 1.7 per cent per year, according to the 2011 Census, and new technologies and skill-intensive sectors have been introduced which have huge backward and forward employment linkages. However, unemployment is widespread, not just in rural and urban areas, but also among the industrial labour, landless and the educated people as well. According to the data compiled by the Centre for Monitoring Indian Economy (CMIE), the unemployment rate rose to 7.2 per cent in February 2019. Since economic reforms, one credible estimate puts the rate of growth of employment as having sharply declined from 2.39 per cent per year to 1.7.

The majority of the labour force is employed in the unorganized sector. About 80 per cent of the workers are living in rural areas, of which 63 per cent are engaged in agriculture, a figure obstinately constant despite a sharp fall in agriculture's share in GDP growth from 50 per cent to 26.2 per cent in 1998. Only 15 per cent of the workforce has regular salaried employment.

Of the working population, only about 8 per cent is employed in the organized sector. About 55 per cent of the total employment in the organized sector is in the service sector and 30 per cent in the manufacturing sector. The share of the public sector in the total employment in the organized sector had increased from 68 per cent in 1981 to 71 per cent in 1991. Since then, the share has declined because of the poor growth rates in employment.

Judging by past trends, unless future growth rate of GDP is stepped up to 10 per cent per year, and the economic reforms redesigned and restructured for employment generation, the country faces the prospects of adding two million persons to the ranks of the unemployed every year and ultimately derailing reform itself.

Economic Reforms and Poverty Alleviation

According to the 53rd round of the National Sample Survey (NSS) data for 1997 (January to December), measured in terms of monthly per capita expenditure, the poverty ratio was estimated at 33.97 per cent in the urban areas in 1997, against 35.29 per cent at the beginning of 1991 (46th round NSS data), i.e. a slight fall during the reforms (See tables 11 and 12). The proportion of the rural population in the poverty bracket has risen in the same period to 38.46 per cent from 35.04 per cent. In other words, taken together, the proportion of people below the poverty line rose from 35 per cent.

Table 11
Projection of Work Opportunities: 1997–2002

Sector	GDP Growth % p.a.	Employment Elasticity to GDP	Rate of Employment Growth	Work Opportunities (million)		
				1997	2002	Increase
	(1)	(2)	(3)	(4)	(5)	(6)
1. Agriculture	3.9	0.50	1.95	238.32	262.48	24.16 (48.2)
2. Mining and Quarrying	7.2	0.60	4.32	2.87	3.54	0.67 (1.3)
3. Manufacturing	8.2	0.25	2.05	43.56	48.22	4.66 (9.3)
4. Electricity	9.3	0.50	4.65	1.54	1.93	0.39 (0.8)

(Contd...)

Sector	GDP Growth % p.a.	Employment Elasticity to GDP	Rate of Employment Growth	Work Opportunities (million)		
				1997	2002	Increase
5. Construction	4.9	0.60	2.94	14.74	17.03	2.29 (4.6)
6. Wholesale & Retail Trade	6.7	0.55	3.685	34.78	41.67	6.89 (13.7)
7. Transport, Storage & Communication	7.3	0.55	4.015	11.96	14.57	2.61 (5.2)
8. Finance, Real Estate, Insurance & Business	8.5	0.53	4.505	4.55	5.68	1.13 (2.2)
9. Community, Social & Personal Services All sectors	7.1 6.5	0.50 0.38	3.55 2.47	38.98 391.40	46.41 441.52	7.43 (14.8) 50.12 (100.0)

Source: Compiled and computed from Planning Commission, Ninth Five-Year Plan, 1997–2002. Vol. I (February, 1999)

Note: Figures in brackets are percentages of total employment in the respective column

Table 12

Labour Force and Employment in the Eighth and the Ninth Plans

		Eighth Plan (1992–97)	Ninth Plan (1997–2000)
1.	Labour Force	374.2	423.4
2.	Employment	367.2	416.4
3.	Unemployment *(1-2) Rate per cent (3/1 × 100)	7.0 1.87%	7.0 1.66%

Source: Planning Commission, Ninth Five-Year Plan (1997–2002), Vol. I, p.190

Note: Estimates for labour force and employment are on usual status concept and pertain to persons of 15 years and above. It does not differentiate between fully and partially employed.

*Row 1 minus Row 2

The uneven pattern of growth during the 1990s could be partly attributed to the reluctance in bringing in Second Generation Reforms in 1996–2007 and yet laud the 1991–96 reforms. A doubt, therefore, prevailed in the public mind on the durability and reversibility of reforms throughout Rao's term as the prime minister.

As a result of this vacillation, economic reform ran out of steam by 1996, and became half-hearted. The reunited and revised Congress party made Sonia Gandhi president. This vacillating approach, therefore, continued due to her dominance in decision-making in the UPA government till 2014, when the Modi-led government was sworn in. But even after 2014, reforms have not touched the really essential areas of states' and city corporations' levels. Till date, deregulation measures have been confined to the Central government, and even here, it has been piecemeal. Privatization, financial institution reform and synchronization with the WTO require changes; however, these have been put on hold. The setback to investment has been serious, causing, a drop of 5 per cent points in the rate of investment to the GDP, and subsequently an unstable decelerating GDP growth rate from 2016 to 2019, which perhaps will continue to decelerate growth.

6

THE MODI YEARS: LOOKING BACK, LOOKING AHEAD

The growth potential of the economy over a medium period depends upon a number of factors. First, the capacity of the economy to maintain a sufficiently high rate of investments and domestic savings. Second, ensuring productive use of that capital investment. Third, the deployment of innovation. Otherwise, the law of diminishing returns will operate and reduce the productivity of capital and labour utilization. Innovations enable moving up the production curve, and not *along* the curve, which exhibits diminishing returns.

The acceleration of economic growth has been examined in detail in many studies. The accumulation of capital and labour stocks, as well as the manner in which these stocks are used with efficiency for productivity in the use of inputs of capital and labour, have been the subjects of intensive study. Global experience suggests that different countries have drawn their growth acceleration in somewhat different proportions from factor accumulation (that is in the use of capital and labour in the production process), which is measured by TFP, a measure of input use efficiency. TFP is the residual that is *not* explained by the factor of capital and labour inputs in production, which represents an array of elements, from technology (both that is embodied in capital and that which is disembodied), to education and skills, to institutions and public policy.

Rapid growth also depends on the adequate availability of labour and the right kind of skills to support it. India has the benefit of a Demographic Dividend because the age structure of the population ensures that the labour force will be growing in contrast to falling in most industrialized countries, even in China. The level of skill of the labour force, however, needs to be enhanced. Skill shortages do emerge as a retarding factor during periods of high growth.

Ideally, we should be able to explore the interaction of different determinants of growth through the use of quantitative economic models, which could illustrate the effect of different policy alternatives. However, it is well recognized that no single model will capture all possible interactions. The NITI Aayog, therefore, relies upon a number of different models constructed by different research institutions which emphasize different aspects of interaction between growth variables. The synthesis view that emerges from this exercise is that it is possible for the economy to work its way out of the current slowdown and restore high growth, but this will take time due to gestation lags and a number of hard policy decisions.

The Indian economy had been, for the last five years (2014–19), planned as the fastest-growing major economy, and projected to grow potentially faster in the coming years than China. However, since 2016, the economy has gradually gone downhill, and the growth rate in GDP has now fallen below 6 per cent for the first time in a decade. The monthly economic report of the Finance Ministry's Department of Economic Affairs listed several factors behind the slowdown, which has not been denied. It is, in fact, widely acknowledged that the growth momentum in the fourth quarter of 2018–19 had slowed to 5.8 per cent annual rate (see Graph 1) due to a string of factors, such as the declining growth of private consumption, a tepid increase in fixed investment and muted exports, all attributable to poor, myopic policymaking by amateurs in the Ministry of Finance.

Graph 1
Economic Report Card: Real Growth of GDP (%)

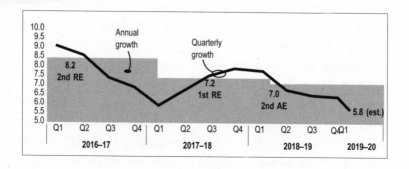

Source: Ministry of Finance report

Note: RE: Revised Estimates, AE: Advance Estimates; Growth of Q4, 2018–19 is implied

Judging by disaggregated macroeconomic data, the economy is on the edge of a 'tailspin' since 2016, and is headed downwards into a serious crisis or crash in the near future. The government's revised data obtained from the Economic Survey (2019–20) presented to the Parliament on 4 July 2019 showed a sharp fall in the annual growth rate of the GDP (see Graph 1) from 8.2 per cent in 2016–17 to 7.2 per cent in 2017–18 to 7 per cent in 2018–19 (estimated) and down to 5.8 per cent annual rate in the first quarter of 2019. Even here, the Ministry of Finance has been caught in an embarrassing controversy on the veracity of government statistics. It does look like a wild hope that the GDP in mid-2024 would be $5 trillion, from the estimated $2.7 trillion in mid-2019. At constant prices, it means a 14.4 per cent growth rate annually.

When an economy is in tailspin, its equivalent 'rudder' and 'Global Positioning System (GPS)' will malfunction. It means that if the tailspin is not rectified, then the economy will hurtle downwards and spiral to a crash, in a zigzag direction. Such a crash in the final stages, often happens fast and without much notice. For example, during the 1975–95 period, East Asian nations such as Japan, South Korea and the Philippines were growing very fast. The growth rates of their GDP exceeded around 10 per cent per year over two decades (1975–95). In the early 1990s, Japan was internationally slated to be able to overtake the US by 2005. *That, however, did not happen.* On the contrary, Japan collapsed financially after 1997 and the US overtook Japan as the buyer of 'spoils' of its failed financial and securities companies. Most bankrupted companies, following the 1997–99 crash (also called the Asian Contagion), thus were gobbled up by US corporates at throwaway prices.

Ironically, the World Bank and the IMF had earlier complimented these East Asian countries for their rapid growth, as an East Asian miracle, in their policy research report titled *The East Asian Miracle: Economic Growth and Public Policy*. The two institutions called their growth paths a 'model' for other nations, such as India, to follow, especially their 'basics' of economic policy. However, the sudden financial blowout in 1997 knocked out these East Asian countries and their financial institutions, and all talk of 'miracle' evaporated (Japan incidentally is yet to recover from that 1997–98 setback). In 2001, the World Bank had to publish an apologetic sequel *Rethinking the East Asian Miracle*.

Closer home, another 'miracle' was 'debunked' by a chosen insider. In June 2019, former chief economic advisor in the Ministry of Finance, Arvind Subramanian (who was especially drafted from Washington, D.C. by the former finance minister, Arun Jaitley), maintained that India's GDP growth was 'overestimated by around 2.5 percentage points between 2011–12 and 2016–17'.[23] This charge remained largely unrebutted by the Ministry of Finance, and was met by deafening silence by the finance minister, whose protégé Subramanian was.

Subramanian claimed that while official estimates pegged the average annual growth at around 7 per cent during the five-year period (2014–19), the actual GDP 'was likely to have been lower, at around 4.5 per cent'. This was most embarrassing for the 'vikas-trumpeted' government, but consistent with my frequent warning based on the Theory of Index Number, i.e., the Samuelson-Swamy research used for GDP estimation.[24] According to Subramanian, 'one sector where the magnitude of mismeasurement is particularly large is manufacturing'. Pre-2011, he asserts, manufacturing value added in national accounts tended to be 'tightly correlated' with the manufacturing component of the index of industrial production (IIP) and manufacturing exports. But post-2014, there is no correlation and is sometimes negative, which makes the official estimates 'incredible'.

Subramanian's analysis is based on seventeen key economic

---

[23]ET Online, 'GDP growth overestimated during 2011–12 and 2016–17: Arvind Subramanian', *The Economic Times*, 14 June 2019, accessed on 27 June 2019, https://economictimes.indiatimes.com/news/economy/policy/gdp-growth-overestimated-during-2011-12-and-2016-17-arvind-subramanian/articleshow/69736248.cms

[24]Paul Samuelson and Subramanian Swamy, 'Invariant Index Numbers and Canonical Duality–A Synthesis', *American Economic Review*, 1974 and 'Notes on Index Numbers', *Economic Journal*, 1984

indicators, which tend to be highly correlated with GDP growth. However, it does not include the controversial MCA-21 database of the Ministry of Corporate Affairs, which forms an integral part of the official CSO's calculation. Incidentally, this ministry was also under Jaitley's charge in the Union government.

His analysis, however, requires to be formally rebutted by the Finance Ministry. The ministry's statement on this charge has so far been intriguing. According to my 'back-of-the-envelope' calculation, a clear and theoretically sound application of the theory of index numbers that Professor Samuelson and I jointly developed would suggest that relying on the official statistics is less than accurate because of the unthinking change of base year for prices. Moreover, without a current NSS survey, the CSO's outdated ratio of output of the organized sector data to estimate the output of the informal sector, with a proper sample is positively ludicrous.

Subramanian's revelation was preceded by another startling admission by his successor, Dr Krishnamurthy Subramanian, in May this year. He stated that based on official statistics, 'there had been some slowdown in the economy over the last two quarters'. He attributed this deceleration to a couple of factors: *structural* (owing to policy) and *cyclical* (owing to ad hoc factors). Besides, he added that there has been a shortfall of about ₹1 trillion in GST collection! This is an amazing admission, considering the effort by the then finance minister in 2017 in the Parliament to claim with great cinematic flair that the GST represented a tax revolution! If revolution means just going round and round (revolving), then that would be true!

Such admissions now by the chief economic advisor are, however, a welcome candour since, over the last two decades, the Ministry of Finance has been increasingly relying on spin, and frequently getting exposed while doing so, thus shaming the ruling

BJP party. The shifting of base year in GDP, unemployment data and impact of demonetization are just a few examples of other disinformation and crude spin. Because of the failing economic performance, the 2019 General Elections to the Lok Sabha had to be fought by the BJP on other issues, such as national security and fighting corruption, and dumping 'vikas' as an election plank.

Is the Economy Spinning out of Control?

We do have preliminary data for 2019–20 to state that the decline in GDP growth will continue into this financial year, dropping even lower than 5.8 per cent annual equivalent Q1 growth rate. The *Mint* Macro Tracker that provides a monthly state-of-the-economy report based on trends across sixteen high-frequency economic indicators, signals deterioration in the macroeconomy in April 2019 owing to a sharp slowdown in growth rates of several sectors of the economy, and a widening of the trade deficit and rising CAD. Of these sixteen macroeconomic indicators, only five were in the green (above the five-year average trend) in April 2019, while seven were in the red (below the five-year average trend).

This is a significant deterioration in the growth rate of the economy compared to a year ago, and suggests that the newly re-elected Modi government in 2019 will need to shape up its economic agenda and focus on measures to prevent this current tailspin from leading to a crash. Moreover, to move to a path of rapid growth, *the government has to recognize that growth in GDP terms has three components*: (i) growth rate in capital deployed, (ii) labour force employment and (iii) technological improvement due to induction of innovations and the quality of skills of the labour force employed, which raises productivity of inputs, and helps to jump to a higher growth path (instead of *along* a current path curve, subject to the law of diminishing returns, that is, less and less return in terms of increased output for more and more inputs of capital and labour).

In a recent article,[25] Dr Rathin Roy, director of the government-run National Institute of Public Finance and Policy (NIPFP) and member of the Economic Advisory Council to the Prime Minister, argued that 'the Centre's fiscal space was severely constrained. It is for this reason, perhaps, that the FM's Budget speech avoids any mention of the macro-fiscal situation. This is understandable: *It has not been the tradition in India to confront such difficulties openly.'*

He further states that 'the total expenditure as per cent of GDP continues to shrink from 13.34 per cent in 2014–15 to 13.2 per cent in 2019–20. Reading Table 1, Chapter 2, Vol II, of the *Economic Survey*, we find that the provisional accounts for 2018–19, as reported by the Controller General of Accounts (CGA), has presented data *that is very different from those* in the revised estimates (2018–19). According to the CGA data, the revenue-GDP ratio is 8.2 per cent, a full percentage point lower than reported in the revised estimates.' (see Table 1)

Table 1

Business as Usual

	2014–15	2018–19 BE	2018–19 RE	2018–19 ES*	2019–20 BE
Total expenditure (% GDP)	13.34	13.0	13.04	12.2	13.2
Fiscal deficit (% GDP)	4.1	3.3	3.4	3.4	3.3

(Contd...)

[25] Arup Roychoudhury, 'India staring at silent fiscal crisis, says PM's advisor Rathin Roy', *Business Standard*, 23 July 2019, accessed on 29 July 2019, https://www.business-standard.com/article/economy-policy/govt-must-consult-before-issuing-foreign-sovereign-debt-rathin-roy-119072201374_1.html

	2014–15	2018–19 BE	2018–19 RE	2018–19 ES*	2019–20 BE
Revenue receipts/GDP	8.83	9.18	9.18	8.2	9.3
Tax-GDP ratio	7.25	7.88	7.88	6.9	7.81

Source: 'Did the Budget ignore the fiscal crisis?' Rediff.com, 16 July 2019, https://www.rediff.com/business/column/did-the-budget-ignore-the-fiscal-crisis/20190716.html

Note: BE: Budget Estimate; RE: Revised Estimate; ES: Economy Survey; * (GA data)

In other words, for the 2019–20 Budget Estimate (BE) to be credible, revenue receipts would need to rise by a whopping 1.1 per cent of the GDP, where the Union Budget allows for just a 0.12 per cent increase! Such spin on finance by the Finance Ministry will land the nation squarely in a massive crisis and a huge credibility loss. But the Ministry as of now is clueless, while its economic advisors seem tongue-tied.

Moreover, the Budget speech of the new finance minister proposes important 'simplifying' reforms. Paragraph 103 of the 2019–20 Budget speech had proposed that the sovereign government of India borrow from foreigners to finance its expenditures. But grave concerns of many of us about this proposal on grounds of economic security and sovereignty, and about the macroeconomic consequences, with no details in the Budget, forced the prime minister to intervene and 'sack' the finance secretary by a transfer. But such firefighting is not enough.

Thus, without doubt, the growth rate of the economy (during 2014–19), calculated on a proper index number-based GDP, has declined over the last four financial years. The annual rate for 2019–20 is, for obvious reasons, not available, but my guess is that the downward trend has not abated. According to the quarterly data for GDP for 1 January to 31 March 2019, the growth rate on annual equivalent has declined to 5.8 per cent, (see Table 2 and Graph 1), a new low for the last decade.

Table 2
GDP at a Glance

% y-o-y	2017 Q4	2018 Q1	2018 Q2	2018 Q3	2018 Q4	2019 Q1
Real GDP (market prices)	7.7	8.1	8.0	7.0	6.6	5.8
Private consumption	5.0	8.8	7.3	9.8	8.1	7.2
Government spending	10.8	21.1	6.6	10.9	6.5	13.1
Fixed investment	12.2	11.8	13.3	11.8	11.7	3.6
Exports	5.3	2.8	10.2	12.7	16.7	10.6
Imports	15.8	16.2	11.0	22.9	14.5	13.3
Real GVA (basic prices)	7.3	7.9	7.7	6.9	6.3	5.7
Agriculture	4.6	6.5	5.1	4.9	2.8	(0.1)
Industry	8.0	8.6	9.9	6.1	6.0	3.4
Mining	4.5	3.8	0.4	(2.2)	1.8	4.2
Manufacturing	8.6	9.5	12.1	6.9	6.4	3.1
Utilities	7.5	9.2	6.7	8.7	8.3	4.3
Services	8.0	8.0	7.5	7.5	7.6	8.2
Construction	8.0	6.4	9.6	8.5	9.7	7.1
Trade, Hotels, Transport, Communication	8.3	6.4	7.8	6.9	6.9	6.0
Finance, Real Estate & Prof. Service	6.8	5.5	6.5	7.0	7.2	9.5
Public Administration, Defence, etc	9.2	15.2	7.5	8.6	7.5	10.7

Source: Economic Survey, Ministry of Finance, February 2019, New Delhi

As Table 2 reveals, the reason why the GDCF in the economy has been slowing down is the *structural* fault. This is a serious tailspin factor that can lead to an economy spinning out of control. Graph 1 suggests that the slowdown is not just of two quarters, but in fact, since 2015—as predicted by me.[26]

The GDP growth has steadily declined from its peak of 8.2 per cent three years ago, as Graph 1 shows. It is expected that the growth of the economy will slow down further to an estimated

---

[26]Subramanian Swamy, 'The way out of the economic tailspin', *The Hindu*, 18 September 2015, accessed on 27 June 2019, https://www.thehindu.com/opinion/lead/the-way-out-of-the-economic-tailspin/article7662610.ece

6 per cent in the year (2019–20), after averaging at 7 per cent for the five-year period 2014–15 to 2018–19. The second-last quarter figure was 6.7 per cent, and it declined further to 5.8 per cent during the first quarter of 2019–20. These trends include domestic demand tapering off on higher borrowing cost due to expected rising real interest rates.

If immediate action thus is not initiated by the new Modi dispensation, it would limit the pace of the economy's growth over the next few years, with real GDP growth of much less than 7 per cent 2020–21 onwards, and all talk of India emerging as a developed country with near-full employment and poverty ratio below 15 per cent of the population will evaporate into thin air. India missed the Industrial Revolution in the nineteenth century, and then lost out in the race for globalization in the twentieth century due to the adoption of the command economy framework, and now is faced with the threat of missing the knowledge and innovation revolution of the twenty-first century too.

The country's investment-to-GDP ratio has remained stagnant at 28 per cent for nearly four years after being 36 per cent for the previous five years. This 36 per cent rate, too, was a decline from a peak of 38 per cent in 2008. If the investment ratio increases a couple of percentage points, it would translate into required investments of nearly ₹3 trillion. The challenge, of course, is that this investment has to come majorly from the private sector, since the public sector is mostly in losses. That would also require urgently addressing debt issues in large sectors, such as power, telecom and civil aviation, and the tax 'terrorism' of GST and Operation Black Money mismanagement that has emerged from 2015.

Household savings, which is the bulk of the national investment, dropped from a high of 34 per cent of GDP to about 26 per cent of GDP in 2017. Non-household savings are about 5 per cent of GDP. This decline in investment rate began even before demonetization, and the decline continues because of intrusive and sometimes obnoxious tax measures. The GST as a practical measure has been a flop, borrowed unthinkingly from the previous UPA government. Despite my sole protest in the Parliament, it was introduced much as a carnival, with gongs reverberating, and the president, prime minister, speaker of the Lok Sabha and the finance minister on stage. Today, we are saddled with redistributed tax revenue collection of nearly ₹1 trillion.[27]

The Ministry of Finance has brutally cut allocations of the investments in infrastructure projects, despite the urgent need for such infrastructure. The economy now needs rupee equivalent of $1 trillion investment in infrastructure to render 'Make in India' a reality, but the actual investment in sanctioned projects is valued even less in real terms than the amount invested in the pre-2014 years.

The manufacturing sector, especially micro, small and medium enterprises (MSMEs), which provide the bulk of employment for the skilled and semi-skilled in the labour force, has been growing at an abysmally low rate between 2 per cent and 5 per cent, and most recently below 2 per cent. The Raghuram Rajan legacy of rising interest rate and falling fixed deposit rate has led to a collapse of the MSME sector, resulting in the rise of unemployment to a forty-five-year high and to a decline in the rate of saving and subsequently of investment to an alarmingly low level of 28 per cent of GDP.

The industrial growth rate has slowed down owing to many structural reasons, including high interest rates, discouraging loan financing of investments, rising fuel prices and lack of credit. The

---

[27]Bloomberg, 'Record ₹1.13 trillion GST collection in April an exception rather than rule', LiveMint, 7 May 2019, accessed on 2 July 2019, https://www.livemint.com/news/india/record-rs-1-13-trillion-gst-collection-in-april-an-exception-rather-than-rule-1557199479905.html

manufacturing sector is progressing at a tepid or slow growth rate of less than 5 per cent per year because of lack of perceived demand, pressure from imports, debt-stressed balance sheets, and more importantly, unwieldy paperwork of the GST that hurt the ease of doing business.

Transaction costs in labour-intensive sectors, such as textiles and garments, construction, agro-processing, footwear and tourism, have risen. Moreover, the growth of eight core industries—electricity, steel, refinery products, crude oil, coal, cement, natural gas and fertilizers—slowed down to 2.1 per cent in February 2019 largely due to a fall in crude oil imports, petroleum refinery production and a stagnant performance of the electricity sector. The overall growth of the eight core sectors in the April–February 2018–19 period was a mere 4.3 per cent. The sectors had expanded to 5.4 per cent in February the previous year. The slowdown is likely to dampen the IIP, as the eight core sectors account for more than 40 per cent of the weight of items included in the index.

Further, plant and machinery assets of the private corporate sector grew by 7.1 per cent in 2017–18. During the first four years of the Modi government, the average annual growth of plant and machinery of the private sector was just 9.2 per cent. Under the UPA-I, it was 19.5 per cent, and under the UPA-II, 13 per cent. Further, credit growth fell significantly and turned negative during November 2016–February 2017. Therefore, it seems that demonetization accentuated the slowdown in credit growth, particularly to the industrial sector.

The significant trouble for the economy today is in the consumer goods sector. Declining automobile sales and poor air-traffic growth suggest that inter-sectoral demands in the economy continue to be weak. Consumers have postponed the decision to purchase vehicles, and the automobile sector was in recession for the financial year (FY) 2019. At 3.6 per cent growth rate expected in the industry, it was lower than last year's 4.4 per cent. Price signals reinforce this alarming picture. That is, decline in the private consumption growth rate has induced recession in the consumer goods industry.

The slowing of inflation cannot be celebrated as an achievement in the absence of robust demand signals and weak purchasing power among the masses. It is a form of deflation. Weak consumer demand is, in fact, crippling the industrial sector. Rail freight traffic growth and core sector growth (reflecting growth in India's eight key infrastructure industries such as power, coal, etc.) are close to the red zone, and currently flashing amber. The Purchasing Managers' Index (PMI) for manufacturing also signals that momentum is slowing, and output is declining for three straight months of 2019.

Worse, the IIP in February 2019 was 0.1 per cent higher a year before. Moreover, export growth over the last five years has been about zero, which has rarely happened in India before. The first quarter of 2019 showed a slight increase, but then the trade balance went deeper into red. The savings and investments rate, which was at 38 per cent, making India among the fastest-growing economies of Asia, has now slid back to below 30 per cent.

NPAs of the PSBs have also risen sharply at a rate of growth much higher than the rate of new advances of these banks, making many large PSBs financially unviable and likely to collapse. Bank credit growth partly reflects the liquidity crunch in the non-banking financial company (NBFC) sector, which has led some NBFC borrowers to turn to banks for loans. This could cause financial contagion in 2019 in all sectors.

India's agricultural products are among the cheapest in the world, with rice, wheat, milk and fruits being in high demand, but restricted in export trade due to the lack of infrastructure—from packaging to transportation to import duties on agricultural products by Europe and the US. This is compounded by our ineffectual position in the WTO in fighting against unjust levies on agricultural imports by Europe and the US. Due to the insufficient irrigation network, we are unable to increase the yield to its maximum potential and export the agricultural products abroad even more. Agriculture is the sector that is the largest employer of India's manpower, but it is grossly underperforming. About 60 per cent of all labour is at present dependent on agriculture for employment.

In fact, the economy is facing a 180-degree adverse situation compared to 2014–15; e.g., a rise in the rupee-dollar rates to ₹70 per dollar, and crude oil prices rising to $85 per barrel, etc., thereby causing a massive crunch for our foreign exchange reserves.

India's foreign trade deficit, as a percentage of its total trade, widened sharply in April 2019 due to a rising import bill (driven by higher crude oil prices) and muted export growth. But since geopolitical uncertainties continue to mount, it is not an easy task ahead. Oil prices are likely to be volatile for the foreseeable future. This would mean India's twin deficits (fiscal deficit and balance of payment's current account deficit) are likely to remain well below zero, i.e., in the red, and negative. Moreover, India's export growth has largely followed global trade growth over the past few decades, and now is at an abysmal low rate.

Even in the one sector where India has a natural advantage— international trade (due to labour-intensive export items such as garments, diamonds and jewellery), we should have been able to expand exports hugely due to the comparatively low salaries for skilled persons in India. Export growth does not, however, happen merely by having low-cost or low-wage labour. It requires well-designed policies based on management of the exchange rate, and on expectations of the same, with intelligent anticipation of interest rate arbitrage.

To improve agricultural exports, FDI would be welcome. But

FDI has declined for the first time in the last six years in 2018–19, falling by 1 per cent to $44.36 billion, as overseas fund inflows have declined in telecom, pharmaceuticals (pharma) and other sectors. According to the latest detailed data of the Department for Promotion of Industry and Internal Trade (DPIIT), FDI (in 2017–18) was a record $44.85 billion. But it declined in 2018–19, as Graph 2 shows. It was in 2012–13 that foreign inflows had registered a contraction of 36 per cent to $22.42 billion, compared to $35.12 billion in 2011–12.

Graph 2
FDI Declines in 2018–19

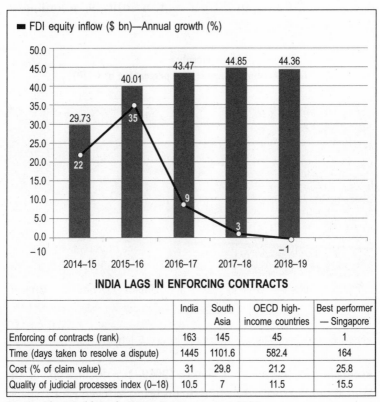

INDIA LAGS IN ENFORCING CONTRACTS

	India	South Asia	OECD high-income countries	Best performer — Singapore
Enforcing of contracts (rank)	163	145	45	1
Time (days taken to resolve a dispute)	1445	1101.6	582.4	164
Cost (% of claim value)	31	29.8	21.2	25.8
Quality of judicial processes index (0–18)	10.5	7	11.5	15.5

Source: The World Bank, Doing Business report 2019

Since 2012–13, the inflows had been continuously increasing and had reached a record high in 2017–18. Hence, the 2018–19 declines are a cause for concern. Decline in foreign inflows would put pressure on the country's balance of payments and may also impact the value of the rupee adversely, for the rate to rise from ₹69 per dollar to ₹75 per dollar by 2022. Hence, resource mobilization has become a cause for concern.

This is contrary to all the hype and spin about GST and more income tax payees put out by the Ministry of Finance. Total receipts (that is, income or revenues) of the Central government—as the share of the GDP—dipped steadily from a high of 9.4 per cent in 2016–17 to 8.8 per cent in 2018–19, according to the CGA (see Graph 3).

Graph 3
Total Receipts [Income] (as percentage of GDP)

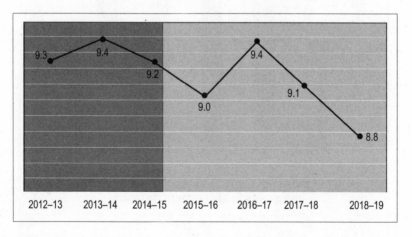

Source: *Budget Documents*, Ministry of Finance, 5 July 2019

According to *Budget at a Glance* (2019–20) documents of the Ministry of Finance, while fresh loans bring in revenue of 19 paisa for every ₹1 of the budget revenue, the government also incurs an expenditure of 18 paisa on every ₹1 of loan received. In other words, the economy is on the verge of a debt trap, which results when repayment of past debts servicing equals or exceeds the receipts from fresh loans.

All these trends put together lead to the conclusion that India's economic growth is tottering, but more crucially, is accompanied by rising joblessness. India usually releases official unemployment data every five years. The government recently published the Periodic Labour Force Survey (PLFS), and delay in releasing it has added to the national controversy around the level of unemployment in India.

The PLFS report confirms the earlier leaked findings that India's unemployment rate is the *highest in three decades*. Coming as it does, just after obtaining a fresh people's mandate, this vital issue of unemployment has put the Modi-led government on the test.

CMIE in a report released in January 2019 revealed that nearly 11 million people lost their jobs in 2018 after demonetization and GST in 2017 hit millions of small businesses, driving them to closure, cut back business and cast a general gloom about the future. According to the CMIE, for the period from January to April 2019, the share of unemployment has risen from an already-high level of 7.66 per cent in 2017 to a whopping 9.35 per cent in 2019, an all-time high. This includes all those who are above eighteen years, unemployed and willing to work. Though the release of official data on this has been stopped, detailed studies from Azim Premji University, CMIE and piecemeal evidence on job announcements and number of applicants in the employment exchange, etc., make it clear that the situation is grim, and needs to be dealt with on a priority basis, which at present is not the case.

How then do we square India's *relative* high growth rate of GDP with these other declining indicators? In terms of pure accounting, some of this is explained by growing inequality in performance. The growth that is happening is concentrated at the top, while the bulk of society—the working classes, the farmers and small businesses—are barely inching forward.

A Monumental Blunder

It is important to recognize that while there have been several good policy initiatives of the prime minister, there have also been major mistakes in implementation, for example, the demonetization of 8 November 2016. There is now a consensus among independent experts within the country, and around the world, that this move was a fiasco and that it had a major negative effect on small businesses, workers and farmers, while leaving the rich virtually unaffected because of the class' ability to rig the system.

It was believed that demonetization would lead to the destruction of currency in the black, that was kept in trunks and silos out of fear of detection. There was no amnesty provided in the demonetization scheme of 2016. Yet, on the contrary, Indians returned almost all the old notes in three months since 8 November 2016. The Reserve Bank of India (RBI) admitted in its annual report that ₹15.3 trillion of the demonetized currency beginning 8 November (i.e. 99.3 per cent), had returned to the banking system. It means that ₹107 billion, or 0.7 per cent worth of the old demonetized notes, was not returned to the banks. By mid-2018, currency in circulation had already returned to previous levels, as highlighted by Graph 4.

Graph 4
Currency in Circulation has Sprung Back After the 2016 Shock

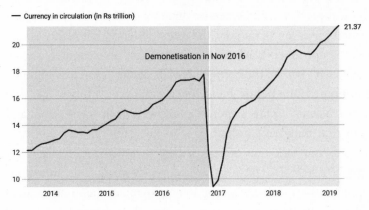

Source: Reserve Bank of India (RBI)

In the European experiment with demonetization, *over a ten-year period*, 99.15 per cent of Italian lira and 98.77 per cent of French francs, had been returned. Remarkably, Indians managed to return 99.3 per cent of the value demonetized in just a sixty-day period. This proves that the evaders and black-money holders had an active collusion for cash conversion with bank officials. The return rate is incredible when, unlike the European demonetizations (which had permitted unlimited redemption), in the Indian demonetization per-person ceilings on exchange of old notes for new ones, the remaining cash was deposited into a bank account. Thus, 99.3 per cent of the currency coming back implies that even though there was 40 per cent black money in the economy, tax evaders and criminals *never held much* of this wealth in cash holdings. The failure to recognize that by the Ministry of Finance and the RBI was an inexcusable implementation blunder of both. Much of the large black money cache was managed through shell companies, foreign accounts, deposits in Jan Dhan accounts, sending the money to Nepal to launder and then again returned to India, or paying temple trusts, cooperative banks, political parties, middlemen or dubious godmen of all religions a small premium to launder the money. Hence, the reality is that there is not much black money in India in unaccountable cash! That is why Dubai, the home of hawala agents, exercises so much disproportionate political and social influence in India—because of its efficiency in black-money conversion both ways—from and to foreign numbered accounts.

The enormous costs imposed by demonetization, viz. over 1 per cent loss of GDP, the near-collapse of small-scale industries, supply chain disruptions, drop in employment, the multiseasonal effect on the crop season and the loss of livelihood due to the government's unpreparedness to change over to new notes, is a governance horror. Demonetization also taught complicit persons new tricks to escape and launder money. *Perhaps this is the main negative lesson.*

But the lesson for structural development remains the same—agriculture needs a renaissance. Even as political outfits compete to win the hearts of farmers, reforms that could have addressed their woes skip the agenda of governance in the farming sector. For example, the economic policies of the government have failed to address the asymmetry between agriculture's high share in employment (about 61 per cent of the labour force in 1991, and 43 per cent in 2017) and low and declining share in GDP (Graph 5) due to poor growth (Table 3).

Table 3

Farm Sector Growth Rate (Percentage Year-on-Year)

Quarter	2011–12 Prices	Current Prices
Jan–Mar 2016	1.07	7.94
Apr–Jun 2016	4.6	14

Quarter	2011–12 Prices	Current Prices
Jul–Sep 2016	6.04	14.03
Oct–Dec 2016	6.82	10.1
Jan–Mar 2017	7.45	11.84
Apr–Jun 2017	4.16	2.78
Jul–Sep 2017	4.48	7.3
Oct–Dec 2017	4.58	9.12
Jan–Mar 2018	6.53	7.74
Apr–Jun 2018	5.07	6.83
Jul–Sep 2018	4.15	3.37
Oct–Dec 2018	2.67	2.04

Source: Central Statistics Office, February 2019

Note: The farm sector includes agriculture, forestry and fishing.

This mismatch has led to a squeeze on agriculture incomes in a sector that is the biggest source of employment for the poor in the economy. Markets have failed to provide relief in either boosting farm incomes or generating enough non-farm jobs, judging by the difference between wholesale and retail prices of agricultural products. The fixer-middleman has replaced the zamindars of the British, resulting in farmers' impoverishment. This is, by far, the biggest challenge to India's structural transformation of the economy. Farm incomes cannot be squeezed indefinitely to keep inflation in check and vice versa. This is the big conundrum facing India's policymakers in agriculture.

Statistics from the NSSO also show that the Other Backward Classes (OBCs) have the biggest relative share in agriculture investment. A continuing crisis in agriculture will inevitably intensify India's caste-empowerment deficit.

As the plots on which farming is carried out have been divided across generations, the average size of these plots has shrunk over the decades.

Graph 5
Falling Significance

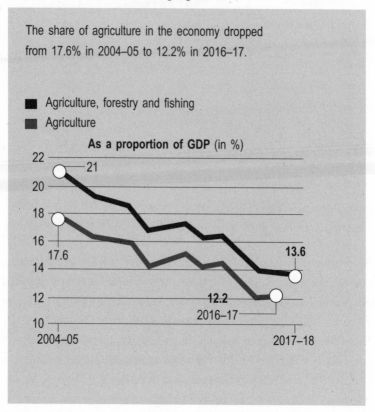

The share of agriculture in the economy dropped
from 17.6% in 2004–05 to 12.2% in 2016–17.

■ Agriculture, forestry and fishing
■ Agriculture

As a proportion of GDP (in %)

Source: Ministry of Statistics and Programme Implementation Report, 2018–19

In 2004–05, agriculture, forestry and fishing accounted for
21 per cent of the economy (see Graph 6). By 2017–18, their
share in the economy dropped to 13.6 per cent. If we consider
only agriculture, its share in the economy has fallen from 17.6
per cent in 2004–05 to 12.2 per cent in 2016–17.

Graph 6
Income-Employment Mismatch in Agriculture Continues to Persist

 Employment in agriculture (% of total employment)
(modeled ILO estimate)

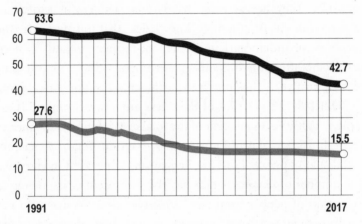 Agriculture, forestry, and fishing, value added (% of GDP)

Source: Economic Survey 2019–20, Ministry of Finance, Government of India

This means that those working in non-farm activities have done much better than farmers. The basic fact is that between 2004–05 and 2017–18, agriculture, forestry and fishing grew by 3.4 per cent every year. The non-farm part of the economy, however, grew by 7.6 per cent every year. But rural wages have remained low.

As a country moves from being developing to becoming developed, farmers move towards construction and real estate. This hasn't happened in India yet. A free market has never been allowed to emerge in agriculture. Hence, the minimum support price (MSP) is insufficient to stabilize the agricultural economy. Other measures are necessary too.

In 2019, even in the case of wheat, only in Punjab and Haryana, farmers were able to get a price that was close to or higher than the MSP. For the remaining rabi crops, prices were close to or lower than the MSP. The same is true for a large number of kharif crops as well. This is what has made farmers angry and wanting to agitate.

Without lease documents acceptable in government records, tenant farmers are still out of the formal credit access and farm subsidies. They access loans from moneylenders at exorbitant rates. While it is common knowledge that farmers are the backbone of Indian agriculture, tenant farmers are still in need of specific attention from the government, which, for the past seventy-two years, has not been forthcoming in implementation.

Officially, 12 per cent of the tillers are tenant farmers. These farmers cultivate 34 per cent of the total cultivable land in Andhra Pradesh, 25 per cent in Punjab, 21 per cent in Bihar, 17 per cent in Odisha, 14 per cent in West Bengal and 15 per cent in Haryana. The number of tenant farmers has risen in recent years, owing to migration of people from rural to urban areas. Waivers do not reach these farmers due to lack of or inadequate documents and Aadhaar-seeded bank accounts.

Ironically, tenant farmers face the fury of nature in times of unseasonal rains and hailstorms. The compensation cheques announced by the government during such times reach the people living in the cities, as the landholdings are registered in their names in the official records, and not the tenant farmers, who actually till the land.

What is also significant is that plot sizes have shrunk. But averages, as usual, hide the real story. The total number of farms stands at 145.6 million (as of 2018). Of this, around 99.9 million farms, or 68.5 per cent, are marginal or less than one hectare in size. The average size of a marginal farm is just 0.38 hectares. In 1970–71, marginal farms comprised 51 per cent of 72 million farms.

It is thus my considered view that the time has come to abolish the ill-fated land reform socialist laws of the 1970s, and permit land consolidation through market forces.

Farming on smaller plots is not as remunerative as it earlier used to be. But it is the status quo in the application of science to cultivation that is the real shortcoming. It has also not helped that the size of agriculture, as a proportion of the overall economy, has come down dramatically over the years. Hence, agriculture requires priority policy focus for systematic reforms and to help it become global in marketing. The next priority focus has to be financing of consumption and then investments.

In 2017, because of excess liquidity in the system that was induced post demonetization, the NBFCs came to the forefront of lending in the last three years because banks were struggling with NPAs. NBFCs thereafter, for example, accounted for 75 per cent of *incremental* auto loans in the FY 2018. The current bad consumer story came to be only after the NBFC crisis erupted. NBFCs now have no money to service the deposits or recover the loans given. The consumption rise, thus, in the past three years was not driven by a rise in personal income (which was actually minimal) but because of a significant rise in lending by NBFCs, which now has backfired.

NBFCs are prohibited from taking deposits, borrowing money (from banks) or transacting commercial papers with mutual funds to raise money. Therefore, in the last few years of high inflows of cash, banks and investors have parked their money with mutual funds. This supply of cheap funds from banks and mutual funds, in turn, helped NBFCs double their loan portfolios.

This economic fault line, therefore, hit credit recovery. NBFCs found themselves suddenly in the mismatch between assets and liabilities, which has led to a downgrading in ratings and, thus, eventual defaults.

With this developing shortage of funds, and hence rising capital costs, NBFCs had to cut credit flow to sectors key to consumption, leading to a crash in leveraged consumption (e.g., auto, housing and consumer durables).

Concomitantly, the household savings rate was partly depleted by increased consumption spending from extended savings. Over the last few years, households had apparently gradually reduced consumption due to insufficient income growth, but could do so no more.

In fact, the biggest hurdle today is that India's aggregate savings rate has seen a large and sustained decline since FY13 (by 4 per cent of GDP). India has witnessed a similar decline in previous downturns (FYs 2000–02 and 2008–10) but those were modest and short-lived. The GDP growth rate's decline since FY15 is largely due to declining household savings, which morphs into investment through financial institutions.

Yet, paradoxically, interest rates have been rising. As per the RBI's release on lending and deposit rates, fresh lending rates increased by 5 bps in April 2019 to 9.8 per cent. This has reportedly led to a 25 bps jump in interest rates for PSU banks. A shrinking deposit base and the declining deposit growth are two key hindrances in effective transmission of rate cuts.

On top of it all, due to fiscal deficit limits, and the likely contraction in revenues, the government will be forced to cut spending—which will lead to a slowdown. India's slowdown is a result of several vicious cycles working in sync, and the nation has no option but to live with it. There is an urgent need for shift in policies to infuse funds into the system. The focus on financing of agriculture must lead to a secondary focus on MSMEs, the sector that employs over 60 per cent of semi-skilled workers in India and produces a host of intermediate products for industries.

A major obstacle in the growth of MSMEs today, with which growth employment is bonded, is their inability to access timely and adequate finance, as most of them are in niche segments where credit appraisal is a major challenge. According to an International Finance Corporation (IFC) estimate, the potential demand for the MSME finance is about $370 billion, as against the current credit supply of a mere $139 billion, a gap that is equivalent to 11 per cent of GDP.

Agriculture, finance and MSMEs have to find priority in the economic policy of the nation. Hence, a recrafting of policy is necessary for a holistic approach to India's economic problems.

Recrafting a New Economic Policy

The economy showed some signs of decline even when Prime Minister Modi's first Cabinet was sworn in on 26 May 2014. Today, after five years, the economy suffers from clueless economic stewardship, cloaked in spin, and media management, while the economy is debilitated by serious multiple structural flaws that make this current slowdown unlike any other we have experienced in India since 1947. Unlike past downturns which were driven by global upheavals, bad weather, inflation, currency volatility and high oil prices, India is today in the middle of monumental structural flaws. It is for the first time since economic liberalization in 1991 that the country is facing a downturn primarily led by a decline in private consumption. The United Nations, in its 2019 *World Economic Situation and Prospects* publication, marked down India's GDP annual growth rate for 2019 as 5.8 for the first quarter of the year based on latest quarter data, making India fall behind a declining China!

If this developing crisis is not dealt with by economic expertise, then a crash is inevitable. The goal of India becoming a G-2 nation seems distant, and well beyond the target date of 2030. While it is undeniable—and a reality—that the economy is headed for a serious crisis through an agonizing tailspin since 2016, *yet the situation is retrievable*. Can a mere course correction today rectify and rescue the economy from a crash? The answer is, yes, of course, but only if there are short-term and long-term economic prescriptions to be followed. In fact, a turnaround can begin within three weeks if the government initiates 'real' economic policy changes, as was done in 1991–96 during the tenures of Chandra Shekhar followed by Narasimha Rao as successive prime ministers when I drafted the reform proposals as a Cabinet minister. We, therefore, need to initiate major economic reforms that are credible and incentive-driven for the people. New Economic Policy, thus, must begin with the reality of the situation facing the country, and on a priority, incentivize the people.

Does the Modi government 2.0 have such contingency prescriptions ready? It does not seem so as of now. The solid grounding in macroeconomics is essential, which Prime Minister Modi and his colleagues in the Cabinet lack. Such Economics-savvy political colleagues cannot be imported. Unless the leader is in sync with such colleagues, which Chandra Shekhar and Rao had been, it is not possible to draft the required reform package and prescription for a government heading for a crisis.

All economic crises have a solution. But the captain of the ship must know which direction to look at. At the present vantage position, I can suggest only one abstract cure: *Search for incentives to cajole the stakeholders in the economy to get enthusiastic about economic activity and be incentivized for it.* However, on a positive note, we should bear in mind that in the last seventy-two years, India has always come out successfully in all crises—once the crisis at hand is acknowledged as such by policymakers, it can then be dealt with squarely by means of reforms that incentivize the people. On each occasion, such as the food crisis of 1965, the foreign exchange crisis of 1990–91, growth renewed on to a higher accelerating path thereafter.

Instead, the first step in the Finance Ministry after the government assuming office in 2019 seems to be to compulsorily retire a large number of serving officers, some of whom were very honest and diligent. This is causing a deep demoralization in the honest officers of bureaucracy. The government today needs a crisis management team of experienced politicians and professional but politically savvy economists who are rooted in the Indian ethos and not compliant to institutions like the IMF and the World Bank to deal with the tailspin that the economy is in. What, however, Prime Minister Modi has constituted is several subcommittees of his ministers, which does not inspire confidence, since none of them have formal training in quantitative economic logic to be applied in a macroeconomic framework, i.e., recognizing the components of the crisis, and identifying the optimum measures that will induce systemic changes, enthuse the stakeholders and monitor the matrix of inter-sectoral impact and trends.

It is important to understand the myth and reality of the current economic situation in order to map the road ahead. The twin engines of growth—consumption and investments—have slowed down. Restarting these engines will require a concerted effort, important expertise and hands-on experience in dealing with the problem. Spin and ridiculing dissenters without understanding the issues at hand will only worsen the current situation. Moreover, Economics is a technical subject of interdependent variables and parameters that allows for objective mathematical and statistical matrix analysis. It is no more a single commodity demand-supply subject but a complex multivariate general equilibrium analysis. Most of all, a concise relevant economic policy must have four explicit sections: (i) the objectives (ii) the priorities (iii) the strategy to achieve the objectives and (iv) the resources to be mobilized. Those in responsible positions who are ignorant of this fact end up trying to bluff or put out a spin and gloss on reality, and getting exposed later, thus losing credibility—as we see today in media debates when government spokespersons participate in them.

An Alternative Ideological Thrust

The present possibility of an economic crash should galvanize the government to honestly review the way we have governed in the past five years, and then rise to new heights with an appropriate change in economic policy, to achieve a higher annual growth rate of 10+ per cent in GDP, with structural changes, which means reforms in agriculture, industry and service sectors. Nothing short of 10 per cent per year GDP growth rate can dent the backlog that is growing annually in unemployment. The Ministry of Finance is merely recycling *ad hoc* microeconomic targets announced by Prime Minister Modi, for example, achieving a $5 trillion in GDP by 2024, or doubling farmers' income in four years without basic calculations. An analysis of the targets means GDP will have to grow at 15 per cent, since the 26 May 2019 GDP level was $2 trillion and the finance minister's absurd claim of $2.7 trillion on 5 July 2019, the day of the Budget speech. Similarly, doubling farmers' income in four years, i.e. by 2022, means the farm income must grow annually at 18 per cent per year. The government has failed to state how to do so, especially the objectives, priorities, strategies and resource mobilization needed for achieving the targets. As of now, without divine intervention, these are impossible-to-achieve targets, a bluff.

The Union government also needs to give an alternative ideological thrust to economic policy rather than try to improve on the failed economic policies of the UPA, as is currently being done with GST, foisting high interest rates, and high tax rates and tax terrorism.

My solutions to fashion an ideological turnaround in the economy and go on the path of a 10+ per cent growth rates are as follows:

i) The individual has to be persuaded by the government through incentives—for example, by abolishing the income tax—and not by coercion, such as harsh levies and taxes. Of course, the state should make no promise to the people without specifying the sacrifice required to be made by them in order to make income tax abolition happen. For example, no consumption binge, savings in term deposits in banks, etc.

ii) To raise the GDP growth rate to more than 10 per cent, the rate of investment, (including FDI) has to rise to 38 per cent of GDP from the present 29 per cent. Of this, household savings are the bulk of India's national savings at 80 per cent of the total. But since 2016, household savings have dropped from a high of 34 per cent of GDP in 2014 to 28 per cent of GDP in 2018, mainly due to the poorly implemented demonetization. The decline in investment and the level of household savings thus cause a decline in the GDP growth rate, a concern that has not been addressed seriously in the budgets of 2016–19.

iii) Households have to be incentivized with the methods mentioned above, viz., personal income tax abolition to raise savings back to 34 per cent of the GDP. We are witnessing today how much unhappiness there is due to income tax terrorism.

iv) Non-household savings today are about 5 per cent of the GDP. For fixed deposits in banks, the rate of interest should not be less than 9 per cent. This will boost institutional and household savings in fixed deposits.

v) Since the growth rate in GDP is calculated as equal to the rate of total investment (as a ratio of GDP) divided by the productivity of capital (measured by capital-output ratio presently at an inefficient high of 4.0), in order to achieve 10+ per cent growth rate in GDP, a household savings rate of 34 per cent of GDP, a non-household saving rate of 5 per cent of GDP and a capital output ratio of less than 3.9 of GDP is necessary. That is, if the rate of investment is 39 per cent and productivity (capital-output) ratio is 3.9, then GDP growth rate is 39 divided by 3.9, which equals 10 per cent. Thus, the higher the productivity in the use of capital (i.e., lower is the capital-output ratio), the higher is the GDP growth rate for the same level of investment. The efficiency in the use of capital is attained more easily by innovations that are introduced by the production technique, and less so by reducing waste and inefficiency.

In addition to dramatic incentives for the household expectation and sentiment to save, and lowering the cost of capital via reducing the prime lending interest rates of banks to 9 per cent, the government also needs to implement a new strategy based on a menu of measures, including:

i) Shifting to a fixed exchange rate regime of ₹50 per dollar for the FY 2019 and then gradually lowering the exchange rate for subsequent years. How that can be done is a huge macroeconomic exercise that space in this book limits me from elaborating.

ii) Abolishing participatory notes (commonly known as a P-note or PN) while invoking the UN Resolution of 2005 to bring back black money of about $1 trillion from abroad held illegally, and

iii) Printing rupee notes to fully finance basic infrastructure and public works projects while keeping especially to pay wages of labourers, and setting aside concerns about fiscal deficit ratio in the cold storage for the time being.

India can make rapid economic progress to become a developed country only through a globally competitive economy, which requires assured access to the markets and technological innovations of the US and some of its allies, such as Israel. This has concomitant political obligations which must be accepted as essential.

We will also have to accelerate growth in the manufacturing, services and exports sectors to wean labour away from agriculture. This will result in higher productivity and income for farmers.

Corporate India expects the government to provide economic stimuli, while the Union Budget seems strapped and starved of funds, facing tax revenue rigidity and debt trap on past loans. What needs fixing as a priority is therefore steps to:

i)   Easing liquidity and tightness
ii) Reducing rural indebtedness
iii) Kick-starting investments in infrastructure projects to promote employment of semi-skilled workers
iv) Enabling increased MSME investment at much lower interest rates.

The first priority for the government ought to be to ease liquidity 'tightness', which affects the entire financial sector by squeezing credit growth, especially NBFC, and threatening the survival of numerous economic players in the financial segment and, most of all, lowering the GCF ratio of the GDP. Demonetization and slower credit growth due to NPAs ballooning on bank balance sheets, with the RBI shifting its monetary policy from a neutral liquidity stance to a deficit stance past October 2018, apparently to keep inflation in check, and the slowdown in government spending to reduce the fiscal deficit, are likely to destabilize the economy.

As far as policy intervention is concerned, we have to break the vicious cycle of simultaneous decline in both private investment and savings rate. On the supply side, the challenge is to reverse the slowdown in the growth of the agriculture sector and sustain the growth in industry. The government will, therefore, have to stimulate the economy by monetary and fiscal measures. These will have to come from radical, out-of-the-box and rational risk-taking on intuitive thinking.

India in the post-globalization craze, like all market economies, is committed to a floating exchange rate system as weighted average based on a basket of currencies. But this kind of floating system does not mean zero intervention by the government.

Going by the World Bank's Ease of Doing Business Index, India has substantially improved in ranking among nations. A significant progress indeed, with its rank improving from 130 among 189 economies in 2016 to 77 among 190 economies in 2018.[28] This should have helped India create more jobs and boost exports.

In the long run, we need to tap the advantages we have in our Demographic Dividend, since economic development theory suggests that more than the inputs of capital and skilled labour, the country needs to raise the productivity of these inputs, which can be done by inducting new innovations in the production process in the form of better practices, new machines and a more educated labour force. For efficient machines and a productive, skilled labour force, the nation needs a Demographic Dividend

---

[28]India Today Web Desk, 'India jumps 23 spots to No. 77 on World Bank Ease of Doing Business Index', *India Today*, 1 November 2018, accessed on 3 July 2019, https://www.indiatoday.in/business/story/india-ease-of-doing-business-index-77-position-1379663-2018-10-31

of young labour, especially those in the age group of 18–40 years. Job opportunities have to be created for them.

Moreover, millions of job opportunities can be created by building new cities. The creation of new cities will be instrumental in absorbing the surplus rural workforce into the construction sector as well as providing aspirational jobs to the educated people in the service sector.

Further, the government-run Indian Agricultural Research Institute (IARI) has demonstrated simple innovations, such as the Green Revolution package, which has led the output per hectare to be quadrupled for most crops.

Research so far has focused on practices for individual crops or enterprises only. The Indian Council of Agricultural Research (ICAR) and State Agricultural Universities (SAUs) should focus on providing recommendation across the farming value chain covering production, post-production, processing and other value-addition activities. India has been blessed with God-given weather that enables three crops to be sown annually, but today only 24 per cent of our vast cultivable land of 120 million hectares has two crops. This is gross underutilization of our endowed land.

Some of the other suggestions mentioned below are presently in the existing economic literature being discussed.

i) The government should convene the Commission for Agricultural Costs and Prices (CACP) by an Agriculture Tribunal vide Article 323B of the Constitution to examine and adjudicate the following:

    • Replace the MSP by a minimum reserve price (MRP), which could be the starting point for auctions at 'mandis' (rural markets).

    • Fight for market access under the WTO for farm output export, for globalization of agriculture and benefit by higher prices internationally for crops, vegetables and milk.

ii)   The government must establish an Agriculture Advisory Service, which would be a technology-driven service on the lines of those of the United States Department of Agriculture (USDA) and the European Union (EU). This would ensure that farmers adopt an optimal cropping pattern that maximizes their income and encourages future trade. States must be encouraged to adopt the Model Contract Farming Act, 2018, as suggested by NITI Aayog as a form of price futures.

iii)   The lack of an adequate and efficient infrastructure of cold warehouses' chain leads to massive post-harvest losses, estimated by scholars at ₹92,561 crore annually. Perishables account for the bulk of post-harvest losses. Moreover, as recent reports indicate, most existing cold storages are single-commodity storages, resulting in their capacities lying idle for up to six months a year. The cold chain infrastructure is also unevenly distributed among states. Inadequate cold chain infrastructure hampers India's food export as well. Countries across the world have stringent guidelines for the import of agricultural and processed food products. The EU has raised more notifications, issued more rejections and destroyed more consignments from India as compared to consignments from other developing countries such as Turkey, Brazil, China and Vietnam. India has huge export potential, reflected in the fact that its domestic commodity prices were below export parity prices in 72 per cent of cases.

iv)   Clearly, agriculture infrastructure, such as rural markets, warehouses, cold chain, farm machinery hubs and public irrigation need upgradation. Warehousing, packing houses, ripening chambers and cold storages, including those set up at the village level, should be accorded full-fledged infrastructure status to enable them to avail the fiscal benefits that come with infrastructure status. This protects the farmer in case of the fall in prices below the MSP.

v) Set up desalination plants along our long coastline to provide adequate water to the coastal states, overcome technological issues and build a water grid by linking major rivers, from the Ganga to the Cauvery, through canals and also develop new alternative technologies, such as hydrogen fuel cells to provide an eco-friendly substitute to petroleum products. Thus, for the coastal areas of India, the much-needed water for irrigation must be obtained from desalination of seawater—this technology is easily available from Israel.

vi) States must be encouraged to adopt the Model Agricultural Land Leasing Act, 2016. This will improve land access to small and marginal farmers through land leasing, whilst also providing for a mechanism for the tenants to avail of institutional credit. A major constraint to land leasing under the present regulatory environment is the unwillingness of landowners to lease out land due to fear of land capture by tenants. Further, complete digitization of land records is a must for effective implementation of land leasing. Geotagging, along with location agnostic online registration of land records to generate updated land records, must be carried out.

vii) Research spending in agriculture, currently at 0.3 per cent, needs to be increased to at least 1 per cent of agriculture GDP. It is essential that new technology be adopted at the farm level. A focus on precision agriculture with support for research on energy-friendly irrigation pumps, micro irrigation, climate-smart technologies, Internet of Things (IoT) and use of technology in animal husbandry to monitor animal behaviour, health and production will help prepare for future challenges.

viii) Through innovation, we must tap our vast thorium deposits for clean electricity generation and thus put an end to power shortage. The government must encourage the use of hydropower in the Northeast.

ix) Thus, another part of the new strategy of growth has to be deploying new innovation, both hard and soft, to enforce the efficiency in use of capital, and thus lower the ICOR.

The world economy after growing at 3.1 per cent in 2017 is now estimated to have slowed down to 3 per cent in 2018, and the outlook for 2019 suggests it will slow down to 2.8 per cent over the next two years. China's GDP growth rate is expected to drop to 6 per cent in 2021 from 6.5 per cent in 2018. India, given its potential, can definitely jump immediately into the 8–10 per cent growth arena. India, thus, continues to be a profitable long-term bet for global investors. We can, of course, no more be satisfied with a 7–9 per cent growth rate if we want to become an economically developed country by 2040, and overtake China before 2030. The Indian economy, thus, needs to grow at 10+ per cent per year for the next ten years to achieve full employment and for India's GDP to overtake China's and pave the way to forming a global economic triumvirate with the US and China by 2050. But it requires informed stewardship of the economy based on a sound knowledge of macroeconomics which is lacking today, thus spreading gloom amongst India's well-wishers in the investor community and its people. India is the only economy that has the potential to match China and overtake it and thereafter, challenge the US in its innovational skills. But only if we try!

Appendix

TOWARDS A NEW IDEOLOGY OF INTEGRAL HUMANISM

In 1970, I had, at the request of a few Bharatiya Jana Sangh leaders such as Nanaji Deshmukh and Jagannathrao Joshi, prepared and presented a *Swadeshi Plan* at the Patna session of the Jana Sangh. This angered the Leftists, since I supported the scrapping of the controls and quota system and the instituting of a competitive market system in place of Soviet socialism. The presenting of the *Swadeshi Plan* instantly turned into a national event. So much so that the then Prime Minister Indira Gandhi, who at that time held the finance portfolio, took the floor of the Lok Sabha on 4 March 1970 during the 1970–71 Budget debate, and denounced the *Swadeshi Plan*, calling its author, namely myself, 'dangerous'. She was particularly irked by my thesis that if India gave up socialism for the competitive market economic system, it could grow at 10 per cent per year, achieve self-reliance and full employment, and also produce nuclear weapons for India's strategic needs.

But my thesis's underpinning was the core concept that

material economic growth had to be harmonized with spiritual advancement. In other words, stand-alone materialistic progress, as in the West, was unsuitable for India.

The core concept is as follows: economic policy designed should be consistent with material goals harmonized with the spiritual values of our ancient nation. It is this embryonic idea that Deendayal Upadhyaya developed into his thesis of *Integral Humanism* and which I developed into a theoretical framework. To quote Deendayalji himself:

> Both these systems—capitalist and communist—have failed to take account of the Integral Man, his true and complete personality, and his aspirations. One system (capitalist) considers him as mere selfish being, hankering for money, having only one law, viz., the law of fierce competition—in essence the law of the jungle. Whereas the other (communist) has viewed him as a feeble lifeless cog in the whole scheme of things regulated by rigid rules, and incapable of any good unless directed. The centralization of power—economic and political—is implied in both. Both, therefore, result in dehumanization of man.[29]

Deendayalji also dismissed the democratic or Gandhian socialism as an ideology failing to establish the importance of the human being.[30]

This is in keeping with the Rashtriya Swayamsevak Sangh (RSS) Chief Guruji Golwalkar's thoughts that class struggle as a concept embedded in all forms of socialism is anti-human; instead, class harmony and conflict resolution are the basic instincts of human beings, especially of Hindutva. Guruji stated that the communist concept of the dictatorship of the proletariat was

---

[29]Deendayal Upadhyaya, *Integral Humanism*, Navchetan Press, Delhi, 1965, p. 76
[30]Ibid., pp. 74–75

nothing but 'the dictatorship of the dictator of a dictatorial party'.[31]

Thus, now well past the centennial year of Sri Guruji's birth, we can say that he gave the nation a new direction in Economics by propounding the concept of integral outlook—namely that economic behaviour must blend with spiritual values to produce a happy and balanced society. We, in this country, are yet to incorporate this redirection in our economic policy, but time will soon be at hand for us to do so when the people's mandate will be given to a new system of governance, and faithfully carried out too. This so far has not happened.

Guruji's ideas fortunately had been incorporated by Deendayalji in his *Integral Humanism* and also by Dattopant Thengadi in his *Ekatma Maanavadarshan*. Thengadi also summarized in point format the discourse he gave in a meeting in Thane, Maharashtra. This was published in the weekly *Organiser* (I am thankful to Dattatreya Hosabale for retrieving it for me).

In 1977, at the invitation of Dr Mahesh Mehta, I presented a paper in New York titled 'Economic Perspectives in Integral Humanism'. This was later published as *Upadhyay Integral Humanism* (edited by Mahesh Mehta himself).

Based on these works and researches, I have written the appendix to this book.

---

[31]See also M.S. Golwalkar, *Bunch of Thoughts*, Sahitya Sindhu Prakashan, 2017, p. 13

However, despite being a colleague of Deendayal Upadhyaya, and successor president of the Bharatiya Jana Sangh, Atal Bihari Vajpayee chose 'Gandhian Socialism' as the ideological platform of the newly formed BJP, which I had rejected. I stayed out of BJP till Hindutva returned as an ideological basis of the BJP. I joined BJP in August 2012.

Structure of Economic Policy in Integral Humanism

The new economic policy is structured in a five-dimensional framework and may be thus defined by: (i) Objectives (ii) Priorities (iii) Strategies (iv) Resource Mobilization Measures, and (v) Institutional Architecture.

Let us consider the first dimension—the objectives of economic policy—for the four main ideologies of communism, capitalism, socialism and integral humanism.

Theoretically, *communism* takes maximum production for the state as the goal, while *capitalism* adopts the concept of survival of the fittest (*laissez faire*)—that of an invisible hand guiding towards maximum profit for producers and maximum consumption of material goods for the worker. *Socialism* aims at maximum welfare measured by social security. The state guarantees against risks of disease, death and unemployment to the individual citizens. That is the concept of welfare under socialism.

However, Deendayalji pointed out that all these goals were purely materialistic and derailed human development. He said that the human being's development must be viewed 'integrally and holistically' (hence the term 'integral humanism'). He advocated the blending of materialistic goals with spiritual imperatives as the primary goal of economic policy. Guruji in *Bunch of Thoughts*, states: 'All attempts and experiments made so far were based on "isms" stemming from materialism.'[32] And then he propounded that 'the problem boils down to one of achieving a synthesis of national aspirations and world welfare'. Guruji advocates that in this synthesis, 'swalambana (or self-reliance) forms the backbone of a free and prosperous nation...'[33], and that, at the very minimum, '"atma poorti" (or self-sufficiency) in food production is a must

---

[32]M.S. Golwalkar, *Bunch Of Thoughts*, Sahitya Sindhu Prakashan, 2017, p. 5
[33]Ibid., p. 313

for our national defence...'[34]

The difference between swalambana and atma poorti is that the former requires us to depend on our own resources; i.e., if there is a shortage of some commodity, we should earn in a foreign exchange through export of goods and services to buy the needed commodity from abroad. In other words, exports support the imports. That is, we should depend on our own resources. The latter concept of atma poorti requires that we produce in sufficient quantities in our own country, so that we do not suffer any shortage. That is, *we should* depend only on our own indigenous production and resources, and not on doles in any form from abroad.

Today we find that the nation has again moved from food self-sufficiency (atma poorti) to dependence on imports. Farmers are committing suicide. Owing to the use of chemicals and genetically mutated foreign seeds, land is diminishing in productivity, some even going barren. Although this is universally true, foreign multinational companies have marketed these untested genetically modified seeds. We must now reorient the objective of our economic policy to regain self-sufficiency in food production. And we must do it through eco-friendly means, such as organic farming, wind energy and the cooperative pooling of resources, and the endeavour for higher output per acre.

Thus the economic perspectives in integral humanism are fundamentally different from those in capitalism, socialism and communism.

Arguing that the so-called democratic socialism is no better, Deendayalji stated: 'Socialism arose as a reaction to capitalism. But even socialism failed to establish the importance of the human being. The needs and preferences of individuals have as much

---

[34]M.S. Golwalkar, *Bunch Of Thoughts*, Sahitya Sindhu Prakashan, 2017, p. 5

importance in the socialist system as in a prison manual.'[35]

Therefore, Deendayalji stated:

> Man, the highest creation of God, is losing his own identity. We must re-establish him in his rightful position, bring him the realization of his greatness, reawaken his abilities and encourage him to exert for attaining divine heights of his latent personality. This is possible only through a decentralized economy.[36]

It is interesting to note that, in 2007, the Congress of the Chinese Communist Party led by Hu Jintao, adopted 'harmonious society' as their party ideology, which in substance is the same as integral humanism.

Deendayalji went on to indicate: 'Swadeshi and decentralization are the two words which can briefly summarise the economic policy suitable for the present circumstances.'[37]

Deendayalji's stress on the need to think in integrated terms is now fashionably called 'systems analysis or holistic view' in the West. He also emphasized the need to liberate man by recognizing 'complementarities' in life. Man is not on his own or alone. Deendayalji's plea for rejection of class struggle and the need to think in terms of conflict resolution and 'class harmony' is much in vogue today in the West, which is getting increasingly disillusioned with capitalism.

The recent trend in the theory of education in the West— human intelligence—hitherto just cognitive development, has been expanded to recognize other dimensions of emotional, moral, social and spiritual innovation, and environmental intelligences for all-round development of the human being.

---

[35]M.S. Golwalkar, *Bunch Of Thoughts*, Sahitya Sindhu Prakashan, 2017, pp. 74–75
[36]Ibid., pp. 76–77
[37]Ibid., p. 78

Thus, if we are not to suffer the social tensions of the West, we have to break away from the path that we have chosen presently, viz., the Nehruvian path that needs to be completely abandoned—partially is not enough for national good. The alternative to materialistic capitalism is *not* communism because even in communist countries there is a problem of 'alienation' and 'exploitation', as revealed recently from reports.

Deendayalji was also aware—in as early as 1965—of the communist degeneration. Logically for him, any system in which man does not receive primacy is bound to ultimately degenerate. Interestingly, Deendayalji quotes M. Djilas, the author of *The New Class: An Analysis of the Communist System* to prove that in communist countries, 'a new class of bureaucratic exploiter has come into existence'.

Thus, by presenting his concept of integral humanism, Deendayalji has placed before the world a new and original alternative ideological framework. To appreciate the fundamentally different structure of economic policy imbedded in integral humanism, I have projected the various alternative competing ideologies in terms of its structural parameters of objectives, priorities, development strategy, resource mobilization and institutional framework.

From Table 1, we may note that the economic perspective of integral humanism is fundamentally different from the other ideologies. Capitalism and communism have similarities in matters of objectives and institutional framework. If cost of production is stabilized, then maximum profit and maximum production are identical.

Table 1
Ideology

Dimension	Capitalism (Adam Smith)	Socialism (Harold Laski)	Communism (Karl Marx)	Integral Humanism (Deendayal Upadhyaya)
1. Objectives	Maximum profit and maximum consumption, Energy-intensive	Maximum material welfare and hedge against risk	Maximum production, swalambana (self-reliance)	Optimum synthesis of national development and global welfare. Swalambana (self-reliance)
2. Priorities	Energy-intensive exploitation of resources	Guaranteed minimum material standards of pay, pension and employment	Primacy of the system based on coercion in the extraction of funds from the people for the state	Primacy of man through balanced development of Chaturvidha Purushartha (Artha, Kama, Dharma, and Moksha)
3. Strategies	Primacy of labour-saving capital-intensive technology, Energy consuming, Free trade globally	Nationalization of commanding heights and public distribution of essential commodities	Total ownership of all the means of production, Foreign trade discouraged	Conflict resolution and harmonization through complemetaries
4. Resource Mobilization Measures	Incentive and propensity to spend, Environment destructive	Taxation and controls and Licensing	Total control on incomes received and permitted consumption, Administered prices and terms and trade	Trusteeship and austerity, Four sources of wealth: vidya, sashtra, dhan and bhoomi distributed without concentration
5. Institutional Architecture	Survival of the fittest, laissez faire in a free market. Invisible hand	Administrative controls, licences and government regulation in a quota system	Dialetical materialism, class struggle and dictatorship of the proletariat	Decentralization, panchyati raj, and self-employment of the people

Again, as stated earlier, class struggle, annihilation and survival of the fittest are different only to the extent that communism envisages the survival of the fittest, whereas capitalism expects the 'fittest' individual to engage in fierce competition and annihilate rivals. Similarly, socialism is different from communism in the extent of coercion and control—only a slight difference, and not fundamentally. That is why communism is often referred to as 'scientific socialism', although there is nothing 'scientific' about it.

Since one socialist differs from another only in mere degrees, there are many varieties of socialism, ranging from those of Hitler's to Uganda's Idi Amin's to Indira Gandhi's to Sweden's democratic socialism. This has only caused confusion and gives ample scope for hypocrisy. Thus, we can see some people in India arguing and debating about nationalization and austerity on the one hand, and at the same time, encouraging foreign collaboration—all the while living in big mansions—on the other. Such inconsistencies can be reconciled in some variety of socialism and interpreted at will.

From the above table, it is also apparent that total humanity and growth of man is nowhere under consideration in any ideology, except in integral humanism.

Humanity as a whole is subservient to these systems, either explicitly or implicitly. Under communism, man explicitly subserves the system. Coercion is legitimized 'in the interest of the state'. Even the choice of career, location of work and advancement are strictly directed by the state. Man in such countries has no room for choice or even opting out of such a system, as his freedom to travel out of the country is completely curbed.

In capitalism, an individual may have the technical freedom for his 'pursuit of happiness', but the system fails to accommodate the varying capabilities and endowments of man. Since the law of the jungle—the survival of the fittest—prevails, some achieve great advancement, while others get trampled upon in what is called the 'rat race'. Since maximum profit is possible only in a newer and latest technology, man has to constantly adjust to the terrifying demands of technology, rather than technology adjusting to the integral needs of man. Today, we witness in an advanced capitalist country, such as the US, broken homes, high divorce rates and ruined family life. So man has to adjust to it or perish. Such a development is inevitable in a system in which the 'shortage of manpower is the guiding factor in the design of machines'.

Thus, in capitalism, under laissez faire, although man has technical freedom, because the development strategy is to give primacy to technology, implicitly man becomes subservient to the system. In such societies, individuality is expressed in other outlets such as crime, free sex, drunkenness and rebel dropout movements. The recent craze in the West for our sadhus and Hinduism arises largely due to this search for individuality, to escape the tensions that this kind of technology demands from the people, and because their own religious preachers are ill-equipped to cope with it.

Just as survival of the fittest is dehumanizing; so is class struggle, which is the foundation of Marxism. Under communism, classes are sought to be eliminated by the intensification of the class struggle. Obviously, such intensification will lead to hatred and tension, and consequently dehumanization. We saw the extent of such dehumanization in communist countries. In the USSR, for example, most prominent intellectuals such as Aleksandr Isayevich Solzhenitsyn and Andrei Sakharov had suffered severe punishment from the state because they had questioned this dehumanization process. In the end, Marxism has failed everywhere, even in the Soviet Union, which has now unravelled into sixteen countries. Comparing the Marxist economic system with market economies of peers, the contrast is obvious.

It is important to recognize that a comparison of countries

with a common history reveals that those countries that adopted the Soviet economic model performed much more poorly than their counterparts who had adopted the market economic strategy. This can easily be concluded by comparing East Germany with West Germany, and North Korea with South Korea.

In India, too, although we achieved a higher GDP growth rate under the Soviet economic strategy than we did under British imperialist rule, it remained at an unimpressive average rate of 4 per cent, from 1952–90, and then to nearly 7 per cent (during 1992–2018).

Thus, the results of the Soviet strategy have not anywhere been commensurate with either the resources mobilized from the public, or in terms of a nation's potential for growth. During the period from 1947 to 1991, the Indian economy had grown at the average rate of less than 4 per cent per year, while countries adopting a different strategy have achieved growth at 10–12 per cent per year in the same period. There is no reason for our low growth rate, considering that we have the world's third-largest scientific and engineering manpower and a high savings rate of 23 per cent of GDP. As mentioned earlier, the so-called 'Four Tigers', namely South Korea, Taiwan, Hong Kong and Singapore, with less trained manpower and limited natural resources, have moved from the Third World category to NICs in just one generation! The per capita income of South Korea, for example, in 1962 was $82, India's was $70 at that time. Today, South Korea's per capita income is about thirteen times that of India's current level!

Postulates of Integral Humanism

I need not dwell any further on the demerits of other ideologies, but consider, in concrete positive terms, what economic perspective Deendayalji's integral humanism offers. I would organize his thoughts in terms of basic economic postulates using modern theoretical terminology and jargon:

Postulate 1: The economy is a subsystem of the society and not the sole guiding factor of social growth. Hence, no economic theorems can be formulated without first recognizing that life is an integral system; and therefore, whatever economic laws are deduced or codified must add, or at least not reduce, the integral growth of man. The centrality of man's divine spark and his evolution is in the four purusharthas of dharma (righteousness and moral values), artha (prosperity and economic values), kama (pleasure, love, psychological values) and moksha (liberation and spiritual values).

Postulate 2: There is plurality and diversity in life. Man is subject to several internal contradictions. The solution is to be based on the harmonization of this plurality, diversity and internal contradictions. Thus, laws governing this harmony will have to be discovered and codified, which we shall call dharma. An economy based on dharma will be a regulated one, within which man's personality and freedom will be given maximum scope, and be enlightened in the social interest.

Postulate 3: There is a negative correlation between the state's coercive power and dharma. In the latter, the acceptance of regulation by man is voluntary because it blends with his individual and collective aspirations; whereas in the former, regulations often conflict with aspirations, and hence, man is coerced into accepting the regulation or suffer.

Postulate 4: A society of persons of common origin, history or culture has a chiti (soul force). It is this chiti that integrates and establishes harmony. Each nation has to search out its chiti and recognize it consciously. Consequently, each country must follow its own development strategy based on its chiti. If it tries to duplicate or replicate other nations', it will come to grief.

Postulate 5: Based on the perception of chiti and recognition of dharma, an economic order can be evolved that rationalizes the mutual inter-balance of the life system by seeking out the complementarities embedded in various conflicting interests in society. Such an order will reveal the system of social choices based on an aggregation of individual values.

Postulate 6: Any economy based on integral humanism will take as is given, besides the normal democratic fundamental rights—i.e., the right to food, the right to work, the right to education and the right to free medical care.

Postulate 7: The right to property is not fundamental, but economic regulation will be based on the complementarity that exists in the conflicting goals of social ownership of property and the necessity for providing incentive to save and to produce.

These seven postulates, in my view, represent the foundation of integral humanism's underlying economic policy. Most of the established and popular slogans of the Indian society emanate from one or more (in combination) of these postulates. For example, the electrifying call of the freedom movement for Swadeshi, or self-reliance, is embedded in Postulate 4. The popular demand for decentralization finds its source in Postulate 3. The modern, internationally fashionable slogan of environmental care and pollution control follows from Postulate 5. The widespread scientific consensus that optimum solutions can only be found in 'systems analysis' is contained explicitly in Postulate 1. Mahatma Gandhi's advocacy of trusteeship is implied in Postulates 2 and 7 together. In other words, these seven postulates can singly or jointly conceptualize and synthesize the various goals that have stirred the soul of India (or its chiti).

With these postulates, we now need to derive the practical guidelines for our economic development. To do that, Postulate 5 is very important. First and foremost, we shall have to list out the various complementarities; second, work out a calculus of costs and benefits to integrate these various complementarities; and third, frame decision rules on how to make social choices based on divergent individual values.

An example of complementarities is that of an orchard farmer who has a honey producer as a neighbour. The bees of the honey producer can conveniently utilize the fruit blossoms of the orchard farmer, with no cost to either but gain to both. This is an example of positive complementarity. An example of negative complementarity is that of pollution. For example, by setting up a fertilizer plant and oil refinery on an extensive scale, employment in that area is certainly generated. But the toxic gases released by these factories adversely affect the health of the public and reduce the productivity of the workers of the entire region. So, overall, the nation is the loser under such circumstances.

We have to select positive complementarities and eschew the negative ones, if integral humanism is to be followed. Therefore, we have to plan our urban habitation system in such a way that toxic material-generating machines are kept far from urban residential centres, or are subject to strict environmental measures, such as a vehicle run on compressed natural gas (CNG) instead of diesel-run public transportation buses. This means our transportation system will have to be integrated with the location planning of industries as well. A good capitalist or a communist will look at the problem piecemeal. The capitalist will choose urban centres because profits are highest there. A communist will also pick urban centres because production will be the maximum where a trained, industrial labour force resides and an infrastructure is readily available. In a capitalist society, the 'survival of the fittest' is the slogan, so there are no complementarities to worry about.

In a communist society, the state is so powerful and coercive that no one questions its decision. In a democratic socialist society, the public will make some noise, so the government will order a few anti-pollution devices to be installed, but urban centres will still be the preferred location in the end.

However, in an integral humanism society, the outlook will be systems-oriented. So the location would be 'optimized', which would not be the urban centre. But a loss in monetary terms would have been suffered by the managers of the enterprise who would have preferred the maximum profit—area of the urban centre. So a 'calculus' of incentives and compensation for affecting the complementarity is needed. Such a calculus is known to economists, but about which, for the shortage of space, I shall not elaborate here.

It is not enough to have a calculus to aggregate the complementarities but also to frame rules on how to make consistent social choices based on individual values. It is not enough to say that in a democracy, social choices should be based on majority decision rule. The format for eliciting this majority needs to be spelt out, otherwise anomalies will result.

For example, suppose we divide society into three groups— A: Agriculturist, M: Manufacturers and S: Workers and those in services. Let us assume that the society consisting of A, M and S has to rank the projects of X: Fertilizer plant, Y: Steel mill and Z: Hospital, in order of preference. Thus, the agriculturist (A) will rank X most important of all, Y second-most important and Z as least important. Therefore, if a choice is offered to them between X and Y, they would choose X. If a choice is given between Y and Z, then they would choose Y. Obviously if X is preferred to Y, and Y is preferred to Z, then X will be preferred to Z for consistency. In notation, I shall write: $\triangle$ for 'preferred to'

Assume: A:→ → X $\triangle$ Y $\triangle$ Z

M:→ → Y $\triangle$ Z $\triangle$ X

S:→ → Z $\triangle$ X $\triangle$ Y

If a vote is taken on each pairs of projects, then we shall have:

X $\triangle$ Y	A+S=2	M = 1	X Y i.e. choose X over Y
Y $\triangle$ Z	A+M=2	S = 1	Y Z i.e. choose Y over Z
X $\triangle$ Z	A=1	M+S=2	Z X i.e. choose Z over X

Thus, in a majority decision without any format, a society may prefer with two-third majority X over Y, Y over Z, *and yet prefer Z over X*! To avoid such social inconsistency, we must ensure that A, M and S consult one another and seek to find out their complementary choices, and then vote.

This is why format and creation of a basic consensus on harmony is so essential. Such a process is lengthy, cumbersome and complicated. But this is the only way to optimize the nation's resources and energies. But the process can be simplified by decentralization of political and economic authority. It cannot be achieved in a centralized society.

Once a decision is taken on the path of development, Deendayalji would advocate incentives and realistic taxation to encourage savings and discourage conspicuous consumption as the only practical way to mobilize resources. This is contained in Postulate 7. Most ideologies are weak when it comes to specifying resource mobilization, perhaps because spelling it out means annoying one section or another. Therefore, the topic is either handled in a general way or indirectly. In the Hindu way of life, man must be encouraged to save and live simply—acquire wealth, but then it must be made socially prestigious to give away his excess wealth or manage it as a 'trustee' for society. In Western societies, the size of a person's wealth is the most important determinant of his social, cultural and national prestige. So, he is encouraged to part with a portion of his wealth by urging him to spend more and on himself! This results in fierce competition about who can spend more on themselves, 'keeping up with the Joneses', thus leading to great waste. In integral humanism's scheme of things, social and cultural influences are integrated into a man's psyche, so that parting with his wealth for society becomes his own desire. In such a framework, there is no weakening of a person's resolve to have his income or pursue its immediate enlargement.

As a trustee, every individual also cares for the physical environment and pollution. He also treats animals humanely.

Now in 2019, India's GDP is the third-largest in the world after US and China. India has the potential to move ahead of China in the next ten years and then challenge the US because of Indian-demonstrated capacity to innovate new technologies for faster growth.

But it requires persons of vision and expertise in Economics to translate such goals into actionable policies—an area where we still find ourselves ill-equipped.

INDEX

Note: The letter '*n*' '*t*' '*f*' following
   locators refers to notes, tables
   and figures respectively.

Aadhaar-seeded bank accounts, 156
Activist-interventionist role of the
   government, 51
Agriculture
   debt ratio, 12
   export, 115
   income-employment mismatch,
      155*f*
   modernization, 81
   performance of, 108–9, 112
   regression in, 38
   research spending in, 169
Al Jazeera, 3
Allocation of resources, 51, 92, 101,
   118
Ambedkar, B.R., xi
American Civil War in 1864–65, 18
Anglophile intellectuals, 5
Aryan-Dravidian racial theory, xi
Asian Contagion, 135
Aurobindo, Sri, 32
Auto loans, incremental, 157
Automobile industry, 46
   declining sales, 144

Average life expectancy, 4

'Back of the envelope' calculation, 3
Balance of payment crisis, 92–93, 95,
   97, 99, 103, 105, 146, 148
Bank credit, gross rates, 113*t*
Banking
   growth of, 115
   nationalization of, 48, 54
Battle of Plassey (1757), 3
Bengal famine, 45
Bharati, Subramania, 32
Bharatiya Jana Sangh, viii, 173, 175*n*
Bharatiya Janata Party (BJP), xiii, 53,
   55, 59, 95, 108, 138
'Big Business Plan', 48
Birla, G.D., 49
Black money, 96, 151–52, 165
   growth of, 39
Board of Industrial and Scientific
   Research, 50
Bombay Plan, 48–50
Bose, Subhash Chandra, 47
British imperialism, ix
   policy of land revenue, 77
British India vs. Princely States, 16*t*
Broadberry, Stephen 6
Budget at a Glance, 148

Bunch of Thoughts, 176
Burma Rice Bowl, 33

Cadastral survey of productivity, 11
Capital and labour stocks,
    accumulation of, 132
Capital expenditure, 46
Capital-intensive industry, xi, 90
Capital output ratio, 89, 164
Capitalism, 176–79, 181–82
Capitalist model, 85
Cash crops, 17–19
Caste brotherhood, 42
Caste-empowerment deficit, 153
Central Statistics Office (CSO), 52
Centre for Monitoring Indian
    Economy (CMIE), 128, 149
Chandra Shekhar, xii, 41, 104, 107,
    160
Chang, John K., 26
Chaudhuri, B.B., 13
Cheap funds, supply of, 157
China
    agricultural performance, 14
    ahead of India, 35
    conditions for pushing
        industrialization, 37
    cultural narcissism, 27
    economic reforms, 64
    'eight reasons' why railroads in, 21
    feudal oligarchy, 14
    GDP growth rate, 170
    growth performance, 91
    growth rate, 37, 64
    growth rate of crops, 14*t*
    ideological disruptions, 36
    indemnity payments to Japan, 26
    indigenous government in, 21
    level of key indicators, 34*t*–35*t*
    literacy rate, 36
    manufacturing output growth, 26
    market reforms in, 84
    occupation of Manchuria, 32

peace treaty with Japan and, 22*n*
railways in, 24
ratio of outputs, 64–65
ratio of rice, wheat and cotton
    yields, 15*t*
starvation and diseases in, 38
victims of imperialism, 26
yield per acre for all crops, 14
Chinese Nationalist Party
    (Kuomintang), 13
Chinese Revolution, 13
Class harmony, 174, 178
Cold chain infrastructure, inadequate,
    168
Colonial administration, 9, 11
Colonial agricultural system, character
    of, 10
Colonial government, role of, 31
Colonial land revenue system, 11–12
Command economy, xiii, 40–41, 44,
    65–66, 71, 85, 92, 105, 118, 142
Commanding heights of economy, 68,
    71, 76, 89
Commercial crop production, 110*t*
Commission for Agricultural Costs
    and Prices (CACP), 167
Common Minimum Programme, 60
Communism, 41, 176–77, 179, 181–82
Communist Party of India, 95
Cooperative farming, 48–49
Cooperative pooling, 177
Coromandel International Limited, 124
Corporate India, 165
Cost escalation, 121
Cost overrun, magnitude of, 121
Cottage industries, development of, 50
Cotton exports, 25
Counterfactual history, 26
Credit recovery, 157
Credit-deposit ratio, 53, 76
Crony corruption, 113
Cronyism, 42, 118
Crude oil price, doubling of, 99

Current account deficit (CAD), 94, 146

Dalal, Sir Ardeshir, 50
Debt-repayment default, 104
Debt-servicing, 94
Default of payment of debt, 41
'Defective Hindu', 30
Defence budget, 31
Dehumanization, 174, 182
Democratic socialism, 177–78, 181
Demographic dividend, xv, 133, 166–67
Demonetization, xiii, 138, 143–44, 149–52, 157, 163
    active collusion for cash conversion, 151
    currency in circulation, 151*f*
    European experiment, 151
    per-person ceilings on exchanging old notes, 151
    slower credit growth, 165
Deregulation measures, 66, 131
Desai, Morarji, 69
Desalination plants, 169
Deshmukh, Nanaji, 173
Destabilization, 25
Djilas, M., 179
Double debt traps, 93
Doubling farmers' income, 162

Ease of Doing Business Index, 166
'East Asia pattern', 103
The East Asian Miracle, 135
East Asian tigers, 89
East India Company, 3–4, 9, 22
    monopoly, 4
    tax collection taxes in India, 3
East Indian Railway (EIR), 22
Economic authority, decentralization of, 188
Economic decentralization, principles of, 84

Economic dislocations, 33
Economic fault line, 157
Economic growth
    acceleration of, 132
    goal of, 29
Economic ideology, ix
Economic planning, consensus for, 45
Economic policy, xii, xiii, 37, 54, 87–88, 98, 100, 135, 159–62, 174–79, 185
Economic reforms, ix, 52–53, 66, 85, 90, 92, 99, 103, 105–6, 108, 115, 125, 128–31, 160
    dimensions of, 126*t*
    poverty alleviation and, 129–31
    failure of, 98
Employment
    double squeeze on, 81
    elasticity, 127–28
    exchanges, 124
    expected increase in, 46
    growth, 74, 80, 124–25
    major sectors, 79*t*
    opportunities, 56–57, 74, 124–26
    slowing down of, 127
Essays in the Theory of Economic Growth, 44
Export
    -import trade, 115
    import and trade balance, 116*t*–17*t*
    manufactures, 115
    vehicle for agricultural modernization, 81

Famine Commission, 5, 11
Farm Sector Growth Rate, 152*t*–53*t*
Feldman, Grigory, 44
Fertilizer Corporation of India (FCI), 124
Finance, growth of, 115
Financial institution reform, 131
Financial institutions, nationalization of, 51

First War of Independence, 2. *See also*
    War of Independence (1857)
Fiscal deficit, 93, 95, 104, 107, 146,
    158, 165–66
Fiscal Management Act, 107
Fiscal reforms, 101–2
Five pillars of transformation, 100–2
Five-Year Plan, 50, 51–83, 90, 100,
    106, 126
    acceleration of economic activity,
        60
    approach document, 55
    better capacity utilization of
        industries, 58
    brief survey of, 55–56
    'course corrections', 52
    dimensions of the states' Plan, 52
    economic setbacks, 59
    employment, 130*t*
    growth performance, 63*t*
    growth rates of investment, 55*t*
    labour force, 130*t*
    original macro parameters, 59*t*
    priority to food, employment and
        productivity, 58
    priority to the removal of poverty, 58
    public-sector investments in, 65
    revised macro parameters, 60
    ritual of a statement of policies, 53
    self-reliance, 57
    separate annual plans, 58
    strategy, 52
    survey of, 53–54
    tempo of development with price
        stability, 57
Food crisis (1965), 160
Food crops, growth performance,
    78*t*–79*t*
Food products production, 101*t*
Foodgrain production, 110*t*
    annual compounded growth rates,
        77*t*
    quinquennium rates 78*t*

Foreign debt, interest payments of, 95
Foreign direct investment (FDI), 108,
    146–47, 163
    declines, 147*f*
Foreign exchange crisis (1990–91),
    41, 161
Foreign exchange reserves, 41, 105,
    119, 146
Foreign inflows, decline in, 148
Foreign loans, repayment of, 41
Foreign trade deficit, 146
Foreign trade, Indian, 96*t*
'Four Tigers', 183

G-2 nation, 159
Gandhi, Indira, viii, 39, 54, 173, 181
    minimal deregulation in foreign
        trade, 105
    'secular Rightist' colleagues, 69
Gandhi, Mahatma, 30, 32, 42, 50,
    84–85, 88, 185
    advocacy of trusteeship, 185
Gandhi, Rajiv, 39, 54, 71, 92, 105
    liberalization measures, 71
Gandhi, Sonia, 131
Gandhian goal of self-reliance, 81
General Agreement on Tariffs and
    Trade (GATT), 86, 99, 114
George, David Lloyd, 28
Geotagging, 169
GFCF, 112–23@
Gilt-edged railway investment
    guarantee, 25
Global Positioning System (GPS), 135
Golwalkar, Guruji, 174
Goods and Services Tax (GST), xiii,
    137, 142–43, 148–49, 163
    as a carnival, 143
    tax revolution, 137
    'terrorism' of, 142
    unwieldy paperwork, 144
Government spending, slowdown in,
    166

Government-imposed controls and
    regulations, 92
Gowda, Deve, 59
Great Leap Forward, 37
Great Uprising of 1857, 9, 23, 31. *See
    also* War of Independence (1857)
Green Revolution, 54, 77, 109, 119,
    167
Gross capital formation, 111*t*
Gross Domestic Capital Formation
    (GDCF), 107
Gross Domestic Product (GDP),
    growth, xi, xv, 39, 59–61, 63,
    67–68, 70–71, 74, 95, 103, 105–8,
    115, 128, 131, 133, 136–38,
    141–42, 149, 158, 162–64, 183
    glance, 141
    higher growth in, 122
    index number-based, 140
    long-term acceleration in, 79
    PPP per-capita, 5, 8*t*
    rapid growth in, vii
    real growth of, 134*f*
    sectoral shares, 68*t*
    by sector, 70*t*, 93*t*
'Ground preparing' exercise, 56
Growth potential of economy, 132
Growth rate of the economy, 89–90,
    138, 140
Gujral, I.K., 59
Gulf War, First, 99
Gupta, Bishnupriya, 6

Harmony, basic consensus on, 188
Heavy progressive taxation,
    proponents of, 91
Hickel, Jason, 3
High-yielding varieties (HYVs), 109
Hindu rate of growth, xii, 68
Hindu refugees, 33
Hinduism, 182
Hindutva, 174
Hoarded wealth, unearthing of, 49

Hosabale, Dattatreya, 175
Human Development Index, 97

Ideological Thrust, 162–71
Ill-fated land reform socialist laws,
    156
Imperialist-ruled India vs. feudal
    China, 14
Impossible-to-achieve targets, 162
Incentive-based market system, 88
Incremental capital-output ratio
    (ICOR), 72–74, 170
    by Sector, 73*t*
Index of industrial production (IIP),
    136
Indian Agricultural Research Institute
    (IARI), 167
Indian Council of Agricultural
    Research (ICAR), 77, 167
Indian National Congress (INC), 47
The Indian War of Independence 1857,
    9
India-Pakistan War (1965), 57
India's ranking in the World, 98*t*
India's relative global economic
    position, 6*t*
Industrial growth, 19, 26, 45, 107,
    112, 143
Industrial output, 101
Industrial revolution, x, 1–2, 5, 8, 142
    innovations of, 31
Industries, nationalization of, 48, 69,
    76
Inflation, 58, 82, 89, 92, 95, 99–100,
    145, 153, 159, 166
Inflation control policy, 82
Integral humanism, 176–79, 181,
    185–87, 189
    postulates of, 183–99
Intellectual commitment, 42, 44
Internal stability, 36
International Monetary Fund (IMF),
    95, 103–4, 135, 161

Internet of Things (IoT), 170
Inter-sectoral balances, x
Investment pattern, restructuring of, 74, 122
Investment policy, 102, 118
Investment ratio, 142
Investment-to-GDP ratio, 142
Iraq's annexation of Kuwait, 99

Jaitley, Arun, 136–37
Jan Dhan accounts, 151
Jintao, Hu, 178
Joshi, Jagannathrao, 173

Karunakaran, K., 105
Key indicators of India, 34t–35t

Labour-intensive export, 146
Labour-intensive sectors, transaction costs in, 144
Labour-surplus country, xi
Land tax, 11, 13, 18
Left movement, 42
Leontief 's Input-Output Analysis, 97
Liberalization and deregulation, 63
'Liberalization' of the economy, 94
Life expectancy, 35, 127
Literacy rates, 36
Loan repayment default, 94

Macaulay's Minute on Education, 31
Maclean, Donald, 41
Macroeconomic view of India's rise and decline, 5
Macroeconomy, deterioration in, 138
Maddison, Angus, 5–6, 8
Mahalanobis, P.C., 37, 44, 56
'Make in India', 143
Maratha Empire, defeat of, 2
Market-driven policy, 88
Market economy, vii, viii, 66, 69, 88, 92, 105–6, 119
Market malfunction, 88

Marxism, foundation of, 182
Mass education, 46
MCA-21 database, 137
Media management, 159
Mehta, Mahesh, 175
Meiji Japan, 31
Micro, small and medium enterprises (MSMEs), 143
    obstacle in the growth, 158
    secondary focus on, 158
Mill, John Stuart, 30
Minerals and Metals Trading Corporation (MMTC), 123
Minimum standards of living, 88
Minimum support price (MSP), 155–56, 169
Minimum wages, 49
Ministry of Electronics and Information Technology (MeitY), 54
Model Agricultural Land Leasing Act (2016), 169
Model Contract Farming Act (2018), 168
Modi, Narendra, xii, 37, 51, 55, 131, 138, 142, 144, 149, 160–62
Moneylenders, 10, 12, 156
Monumental blunder, 150–59. See also Demonetization
Monumental error, 38
Moral degeneration, 92
Morris, Morris D., 26
Mueller, Max, xi
Multiparty democracy, 90
Multiple cropping, 17
Multiplier effect on growth, 111

Naoroji, Dadabhai, 2, 30, 32
Narayan, Jayaprakash, 84
National Accounts, 106
National Development Council (NDC), 52
National Institute of Public Finance

and Policy (NIPFP), 139
National Planning Committee (NPC), 47
National Renewal Fund (NRF), 125
National Sample Survey (NSS), 125, 129, 137
'Natural vital resource', xv
Negative developments, 98–99
Nehru, Jawaharlal, 37, 39, 47–48, 69
   'socialist pattern' of society, 69
Nehruvian Socialism, 51–83. *See also* Five Year Plans
Neogy, K.C., 50
Neo-landed moneylender, 19
The New Class, 179
New Economic Policy, recrafting, 159–62
Newly Industrialized Countries (NIC), 66
NITI Aayog, 55, 133, 168
Non-banking financial company (NBFC), 145, 157–58
Non-farm activities, 155
Non-food crops, growth performance, 78*t*–79*t*
Non-performing assets (NPAs), 113, 165
NRI deposit, 94, 99

Oil and Natural Gas Commission (ONGC), 123
Oil import bill, 99
Oil prices, 146
Operation Black Money, 142
Organic farming, 177
Oriental Spinning and Weaving Mill, 27
Overambitious goals, viii

Panchayat, collective responsibility, 11
Parliamentary Research Service (PRS), 53
Participatory notes (P-note or PN), 164

Patel, Sardar, 42, 84, 88
Patnaik, Utsa, 2, 4
People's Plan, 49–50. *See also* Roy, M.N.
Periodic Labour Force Survey (PLFS), 149
Perishables account, 168
Petit, Sir Dinshaw Maneckji, 27
Philby, Kim, 41, 43
Planned and Actual Sectoral Public Investment, 109*t*
Planned Economy for India, 45
Planning Commission, 51–53, 55. *See also* NITI Aayog
Political authority, decentralization of, 188
Population and labour force, 125*t*, 127*t*
Population growth, high rate of, 124
Poverty alleviation, 129–31
Poverty and Un-British Rule in India, 2
PPP-adjusted per capita income, 7
Princely states, ix, 4, 15–16, 25, 50
Printing rupee notes, 165
Private sectors, gross capital formation, 111*t*
Private-sector-investment portfolio, 123
Privatization, 118, 131
Programme Evaluation Organisation (PEO), 52
Progressive taxation, vii, 91
Protectionist policies, 107
Public Accounts Committee (PAC), 120
Public distribution system (PDS) subsidies, 119
Public investment allocation, 30
Public saving, 71–72, 121
Public-sector
   gross capital formation, 111*t*
   investment, 90

savings, 72, 122
Public-sector corporations, 121
Public-sector undertakings (PSUs),
   86, 119
   subsidization of, 119
Punjab Land Alienation Act (1900), 17
Purchasing Managers' Index (PMI) for
   manufacturing, 145
Purchasing power, lack of, 72
Purchasing Power Parity (PPP), xiv

Qing dynasty, 13, 18
Quality of life, xiv, xv, 74, 100
   indicators, 97
Quantitative Economic Logic, 161
Queen Victoria, 9

Racism, 32
Rail freight traffic growth, 145
Rajagopalachari, C., 43, 88
Rajan, Raghuram, 143
Ranade, Mahadev Govind, 31
Rani of Jhansi, 2, 9
Rao, P.V. Narasimha, ix, xi, 54, 59,
   65–66, 86, 105, 107, 160
Rashtriya Swayamsevak Sangh (RSS),
   174
'Rat race', 182
Real estate, growth in, 115
Real public investment, declining, 80
Real wages in the selected sectors, 83t
Reform movement, 84
Reserve Bank of India (RBI), 150
Resource mobilization, 148, 162, 179,
   188
Resource utilization, 122
Rethinking the East Asian Miracle, 136
Right to property, 185
Rostow, Walt Whitman, 33
Roy, M.N., 49
Roy, Raja Ram Mohan, 31
Roy, Rathin, 139
Rupee-dollar rates, 146

Rural wages, 155
Russian invasion of India, British
   concern, 30

'Safety net', 118
Sakharov, Andire, 182
Samuelson-Swamy research, 136
Sanskrit-medium schools and
   universities, 32
Saraswati, Swami Dayanand, 31
Savarkar, Veer, 9
Savings-investment gap, 94
'Scientific' agriculture in Europe, 10
Scientific socialism, 181
Second generation reforms, 66, 131
Sectoral growth rates, 67
Service sector, growth of, 114–15
Shah, K.T., 47
Shastri, Lal Bahadur, 54, 77
Singh, Arjun, 105
Singh, Charan, 43, 84
Singh, Manmohan, xii
Singh, V.P., 95, 104–5
Sino-Japanese War, first, 22n
Skill shortages, 133
Slow industrialization, 29
Smith, Adam, 43
Socialism, vii, 69, 90–91, 131, 173–74,
   176–77, 181
Socialist oligarchic dogma, 42
'Socialist pattern' of society, 44
Socialist Soviet model, 38
Software exports, 115
Software revolution, 119
Solzhenitsyn, Aleksandr Isayevich, 182
South/North Korea, economic
   indicators, 61t–62t
Soviet command economy model,
   ix, 44
Soviet economic model, 20, 36, 56,
   61, 75, 82, 85, 100, 183
Soviet economic strategy, 52–54,
   63–64, 71, 76, 84–85, 183

indictment of the, 71
Soviet-inspired economic strategy, 42
Soviet model plan period (1952–91),
  102
Soviet style industrialization, 77
Stages of Economic Growth, 33
Standard of living, rise in, 51
State Agricultural Universities (SAUs),
  167
State-directed economic planning, 42
State intervention, 71
State Trading Corporation (STC), 123
Statistical matrix analysis, 161
Steel Authority of India Limited
  (SAIL), 123
Structural change, 108–29
  bank credit and loans, 112
  deceleration in industrial
    investment, 112
  infrastructural bottlenecks, 113
  performance of agriculture, 112
  tariff reduction, 114
  WTO-induced lower-cost imports,
    114
Structural fault, 141
Subramanian, Arvind, 136
Subramanian, Krishnamurthy, 137
'Survival of the fittest', 176, 181–82,
  187
Swadeshi Plan, viii, 173
Swaminathan, M.S., 77

Tagore, Dwarkanath, 22
Taiping Rebellion, 15, 18
Tata Iron and Steel Company Limited
  (TISCO), 124
Tata, J.R.D., 49
Tata, Jamsetji, 28
Tax terrorism, 142, 163
Tax-and-buy system, 4
Tax-collecting machinery, 91
Tea and coffee plantations, 27
'Ten Urgent Requirements' for the

economy. See Visvesvaraya, M.
Tenants-in-cultivation, 12
Tenant farmers, 156
The Hindu, xi, xii
Theory of Index Number, 136
Third World, 51, 66, 183
Tilak, Bal Gangadhar, 30
Tiwari, N.D., 105
Total Factor Productivity (TFP), 111,
  133
Total receipts, 148f
Trade deficits, 115
Trade reform, 104
Traffic intensity ratio, 24
Treaty of Lahore in 1846, 17
Treaty of Shimonoseki, 22
Triggers, 92–100

Unaccounted-for cash, 96
Unemployment, 90, 128
  goal of reducing, 126
Uneven pattern of growth, 131
United Front government, 60
United Nations Development
  Programme (UNDP), 97
United Nations Economic and Social
  Commission, 97
United States Department of
  Agriculture (USDA), 168
UPA government, xii, 60, 107, 131,
  143–44
  failed economic policies, 162
Upadhyaya, Deendayal, 88, 174–79,
  188
  integral humanism, 184
Uruguay round, 76

Vajpayee, Atal Bihari, viii, 59, 107,
  175
'Vikas-trumpeted' government, 136
Visvesvaraya, M., 30, 46–47
Vivekananda, Swami, 32

War of Independence (1857), 15,
    23–24
West/East Germany, economic
    indicators, 61t–62t
Wind energy, 177
Work opportunities, projection of,
    129–30
World Bank, 8, 79, 111, 135, 161, 166
World Economic Situation and
    Prospects, 159
World Trade Organization (WTO),
    76, 86, 99, 114, 131, 146

World War I, 3, 7, 12, 18, 26, 28, 31
World War II, 3, 18–19, 31–33, 47,
    50, 131

Xiaoping, Deng, 24, 90
Xinhai Revolution, 13

Zamindars, ix, 3, 10, 44, 153
Zamindari, abolition of, 43
Zamindari system, 3, 10, 18